THE HILLS OF MAINE
And Other Stories

THE HILLS OF MAINE

And Other Stories

by WILLIAM M. CLARK

NORTH COUNTRY PRESS
■ UNITY, MAINE ■

Publisher's Acknowledgement: This book could not have been compiled without the sensitive, gracious assistance of Betty Clark, the author's wife and companion for 15 years. Her presence also is within these pages.

Library of Congress Cataloging-in-Publication Data

Clark, Bill, 1913–1988.
    The hills of Maine: and other stories/ by Bill Clark
        p.   cm.
    ISBN 0-945980-17-5 (pbk.) : $12.95 (est.)
    1. Maine—Fiction. I. Title.
P53553. L273H55   1989
813'.54—dc20   89-28250
                                          CIP

Portions of this book first appeared in the Portland Press Herald.
"The Hills of Maine—Source of Rivers and Men" is reprinted from *New England Galaxy,* Fall 1969 © Old Sturbridge, Inc. Used by permission.
"Foreclosure Man" is reprinted from *The Saturday Evening Post* ©1960 The Curtis Publishing Co.

Cover photograph by Richard V. Procopio.
Designed and edited by Heidi N. Brugger.
Composition by Camden Type 'n Graphics, Camden, Maine.
Manufactured in the U.S.A. by Maple-Vail Book Manufacturing Group, York, Pennsylvania.
No part of this book may be reproduced or transmitted in any form or by any means, electronic or mechanical, including photocopying, recording or by any information storage and retrieval system, without the written permission of the publisher, except by a reviewer quoting brief passages in a magazine, newspaper, or broadcast. Address inquiries to North Country Press, P.O. Box 440, Belfast, ME 04915.

To the grandchildren—
Polly, Andy, Jennifer, Mary Ann, Douglas, Katie Jean,
Scott, Sara, Ben

Contents

Preface
by Jim Brunelle

As a writer, Bill Clark was something of a late bloomer, taking it up seriously only in middle age. The idea for the column about Maine woods and forestry conservation came to him while he was working in a sawmill. "I was foreman of a mill at Saco," he recalled, "and I got so hot under the collar at the good wood log cutters brought us and sold at junk-wood prices—ash, maple, yellow birch—that I wrote a piece about some of the stupidities in thoughtless woodcutting."

In the fall of 1957, the first of Clark's "Logrolling" columns, later called "Some Logrolling," began appearing each Friday in the *Portland Press Herald.* It was intended to be no more than an informed, folksy series on woodland management for the paper's "Living in Maine" page. The style was tentative, even awkward at first, but quickly took on an ease and confidence that stayed with his work for the rest of his life. If there is a seamlessness to the earliest and latest material found in this book [including the previously unpublished "Please Respect the Residents"], it is because Clark found his natural writing style early and stuck with it.

Once he got started at writing, he threw himself into it with the same good-natured intensity with which he tackled every fresh stage of his variegated life. He worked hard—at one point he was producing an incredible seven columns a week—turning out two or three drafts of every piece before he was satisfied. A 1967 newspaper feature described his rewriting habits aptly, if somewhat perplexingly: "He averages about 5,000 original words a day. In addition, he will write another 7,000 to 8,000 words."

If he had chosen to be an artist instead of a writer, he would have been a top-notch caricaturist. His feel for the comic line was sure, his instinct for deft exaggeration turned the ordinary into the genuinely funny. In this he was heir to a national literary tradition routed deeply in the soil of this New England state.

Modern American political humor was born in Maine in the early 19th century, with the invention of "Major Jack Downing" by Portland newspaperman Seba Smith. The Downing character was essentially that of a rustic innocent whose wide-eyed observations of the passing scene allowed Smith to poke fun at the political leaders of the day without giving particular offense either to his victims or their followers. It was an approach—still employed by such writers as Art Buchwald and Russell Baker—that allowed just about everybody to share in the fun.

Created as a means of lampooning the foibles of the Maine Legislature, Downing went on to become an immensely popular national comic figure with satirical commentaries on the presidential administration of Andrew Jackson. It was the first truly American literary satire, using localized characters and characteristics as a device for commenting on political, social, and cultural developments of the day.

Clark followed the Seba Smith mold by introducing the inhabitants of a fictional Maine town to carry on his own pointed discussion of current events. Gradually the denizens of Cedar River—Francis Gage, Doc Yates, Florence Coosterman, Jonas P. Hall, and the Uncles Waldron, Oscar, and Jake—emerged to give flesh and mirth to the "Logrolling" columns.

The Cedar River folk sprang from reality, from the dozen or so communities where Clark had spent time as a boy and man, logger, cabinetmaker, schoolteacher, husband, restauranteur, bulldozer operator, poet, electrician, selectman . . . whatever. The column shifted in tone from instruction to opinion and soon moved over to the editorial page, where it became a fixture for three decades.

Clark was decidedly conservative in outlook, but he could not abide zealotry in any form. He treated political eccentrics in kindly fashion but was thoroughly impatient with political extremists, even those who shared his views. He mistrusted with equal fervor government bureaucrats and true believers in anything who couldn't laugh at themselves.

Today Cedar River is ripe for rediscovery, which is one of the joys of a book like this. It reminds us that Clark's fictional Maine community was—and indeed is—every bit as rich a locus of American mythology as Spoon River or Winesburg, Ohio or Lake Wobegon.

Clark always prided himself on being a chronicler of rurality rather than just another Downeast humorist. He was openly contemptuous of many of the state's well-known comic writers, storytellers, and performers because he felt they ridiculed the rural folk of Maine and dishonestly played them for cheap laughs.

He had far more respect for the new realists among Maine writers—Carolyn Chute and others of the Erskine Caldwell school of narrative—but was perplexed by their relentlessly dour portraits of the backwoods poor. (Despite his Scottish heritage, his outlook on life was basically sunny.) He felt a kinship with these writers in terms of subject matter, but where their characters may seem to be more harshly true to life, his are more identifiably human and warm-blooded.

Just turn randomly to any page in this book and begin to read. You'll see.

—Cape Elizabeth
April 1990

Editor's note: For those of you who would like to read more of Bill Clark's Cedar River tales, his last book in that series, *Sing Peace to Cedar River* (Guy Gannett Publishing Co., 1982), is still available. *Over t' Home & From Away: Best of Maine Humor* (Guy Gannett Publishing Co., 1980), edited by Jim Brunelle, has a lengthy excerpt from Bill's *Tales of Cedar River*; it is also currently in print.

The Hills of Maine—
Source of Rivers and Men

We had driven up the river, past the old farms in neglect, past the fields where the trees were crossing the once firm lines of the fences. We passed the silent village and we came to the farmhouse which all the scattered family still considered home.

My country was a hundred miles away, but it was in kindred hills with kindred traditions, so I knew what to expect, and although I knew what kind of a family it was, it knew little about me.

So at noontime we sat around the big table in the farmhouse kitchen. There was cob-smoked ham, fried in thin slices. There was chicken, pried from its bones and stewed. There were Saturday's beans in a crusted crock, and biscuits made with thick cream. There were green beans in buttered milk and there were potatoes and pickles and pie and homemade cheese. There was much plate passing and little talk.

People sifted in, people from other farmhouses up and down the road, men and women, family and friends. They refused food and took sidewall chairs. They looked. They looked at the boy, at the boy who was I. They looked at "Idelle's daughter's young man."

They looked because the looking was expected, because that was the way things were done. It was not a question of interference or of forbidding. It was a question of courtesy, of a pattern that seemed worth keeping. Their generation was fading and mine was coming of age, but my generation, though it would

1

have resented interference, was still looking for approval, was willing to be surveyed.

Thirty years ago, while the newly mature were ready to challenge the traditions of the past and to make revisions of the social and moral codes that sometimes seemed stifling, they did not challenge families as families, because they knew that there could be a comfort in being regarded as a friend instead of as "that one . . . you know . . . that Dorothy married."

In the kitchen in which I sat, one man's approval seemed important. His relationship was indefinable. He was not a relative at all, but he was looked to for support and assurance. His name was Alanson Hunnewell and he seemed to be the one who would decide.

That decision would decide nothing, really, and yet it would decide everything. Complexity was not born with Suburbia.

No one was in a hurry in that kitchen. The people knew no schedule except that of need. We sat in the mingled smell of wood smoke and coffee and food. We all gave short answers to short questions. None of the questions was specific. None was vital. All were concessions to companionship. But Alanson Hunnewell pondered each reply as though he were assuring the questioner that his interest was held.

Alanson had clear eyes and a tanned face with a lighter area above the forehead line of countless hats. At four o'clock he reached for his denim jacket, nodded to me, and said, "Like to help with the chores?"

I would have done anything to get out of that kitchen.

We portioned out hay and grain. We spoke gently to cows and horses as they were fed and milked. Alanson stroked a sleek heifer but he avoided friendship sought by two bull calves in a pen.

"Veal shortly," he said. I understood. The condemned must not be caressed.

Cats came to the separator and sows came to their troughs. We chewed strands of sweet hay as we carried wood. We tended sheep. Finally Alanson barred the big double doors of the upper barn with a close grained piece of plank, newly planed.

"Picked that up at the mill the other day," he said. "Nice looking oak, ain't it?"

It was a trifling thing on which to judge a man, but he didn't have much else. I did the best I could, mixing politeness with truth.

"It is if you say so," I replied. "Of course the oak tree it came from must have startled folks a bit."

Alanson cocked his head and one eyebrow rose. "How's that?" he asked.

I kept my face straight and looked into the clear eyes. "On account of having beechnuts on it," I explained.

Alanson spat out the hay strand and laughed. Alanson laughed well. His laugh had brotherhood in it. I laughed with him. We laughed together. Then Alanson stuck out his hand. This time it wasn't a meeting gesture.

"You come again," he said. "Come anytime."

The road was much prettier on the drive home than it had been in the morning. I couldn't see the side hills or the streams or the old headers rotting at the edges of the pastures, but the road was prettier, just the same.

In the years that followed, my generation began to be pushed in its turn. My generation began to age. Five more years of depression helped, and a war helped, and the gasps of the gut-shot dying helped the ageing even more. But whenever I could, I went back to that farm. Every time I went, I learned. Alanson never claimed to be a teacher, but he taught. He taught the truths he knew, because he didn't want them lost. He knew a lot of truths. He didn't hammer them at anyone. He laid them on the counter to be picked up. He told them in stories.

Alanson was a storyteller. He remembered. He grew up while the Civil War was still vivid in men's minds, while the covered wagons were still heading for the west. The Kennebec Valley was fostering farms that supported churches and schools and roads. The land was strongly peopled. Men laid their hay away in the summer heat and plodded in procession with the oxen into the woods each fall. The oxen fared better than the men. The oxen were more valuable.

With a few words and a wave of his hand, Alanson could
sound the echoes of the axes in the hills and the bells of sheep
in the pastures. He could build the old cook fires on the riverbank and sag the planks of the crowded dance hall floor. He
pictured the river-drive days, logs crossed and twisted forty
feet in the air, night camps with men eating in the rain and
crawling under sodden comforters on the wet ground to sleep.
He told of men buried in the eddies, of gashed legs plastered
with tobacco and bound with rags. Misery came out in his
stories, the ache of tired muscles, the blunders of weary men.
But pride came out, too, pride and remembered courage.

Alanson never lost that courage. As he grew older, the people
thinned out. His farm became an island. The hotel closed. The
barns fell down. The stores did less and less trade. The village
drew itself into a tighter and tighter circle. The power lines
came in when most of the users were past the use. Only the
cemetery grew.

By the time Alanson was eighty years old, every single thing
in his area that he had considered sane and solid and lasting
was gone. He might have been expected to devote himself to
nostalgia.

But he didn't. He didn't want to sit and remember. He wanted
to observe. He made fun of the men, younger than he, who
complained about the laziness and the worthlessness of the
newly mature.

"Old Abel Turner," he chuckled, "thinks the world come to an
end when the blacksmith shop closed down. There was more
time wasted in a blacksmith shop than there is now in Washing-
ton, D.C. Five or six men stood around while another man
worked. Abel groans about the folks who run the roads so
much. He says the roads is too good and cars is too plentiful.
But, Bill, that ain't why the people are running the roads. They
run the roads because they're the kind of people who used to
hang around in the blacksmith shop."

A magazine man came with a camera to take some pictures
of the old axe mill, closed and falling apart. Alanson stopped to
watch, and the magazine man smiled and voiced some pity that

the place had changed. Alanson led him to the side of the road and pushed the weeds away from a big grindstone. It was eight inches thick and four feet in diameter. He kicked at it and he laughed.

"Sure we hated to lose the factory," he said, "but, mister, men shouldn't have to work as hard as them fellows did, just to make an axe. Now this stone lets you see what they were up against. My father brought this stone here. My father was a teamster. The fellow that run this factory, he wore out three or four of them grindstones a year. The stones come from France. They weighed a solid ton."

"I can believe it," said the magazine man.

"Well, there was this stone at the railhead in Skowhegan and the factory owner needed it. My father promised he'd bring it on his next trip. But when he backed up to the station platform, the agent told him that the stone was cracked. The agent said it was the railroad's fault and they'd make good, but there wasn't any sense in taking the stone any further. My father didn't see it that way. He'd promised to bring that stone, so he brought it. He brought a ton of useless stone thirty-four miles over dirt roads, to lay here in the weeds forever. He done his duty. But that don't mean it was smart."

"I see what you mean."

"No, you don't," said Alanson, "because I don't know what I mean myself."

After the war, when the peace seemed a worse fear than the fighting, I came for a three-day stay with Alanson Hunnewell. It was November, close to the end of the year, close to the end for the old farmer who had seen so much.

We drove to the river bend, and we walked through the woods to the bank, and we talked of blueberries and bears and television and work. We started back and the heater came on.

"There you are," said Alanson. "You step out of the cold and in five minutes you're warm. We had to walk brisk on the way home. It would be getting dark, and the house lamps looked good. But we were hungry enough to eat gravy poured over an old dishrag."

"You like to look at the good things now," I said, "but honestly, from everything you've said, taking in morals and honesty and worries and a chance to get ahead, I think I'd rather have lived in the older days."

"No you wouldn't. You'd get just as tired of salt fish and pork and beans and frozen potatoes and molasses as any of the rest of us. Molasses. I've et enough molasses to float the drive from Dead River to Skowhegan."

He opened the car door. We were back at the farm. "One thing I will say, though," he admitted. "People weren't afraid. A drive crew could take the trickle out of a sap spout and bring a few thousand feet of logs to the mill. A farmer could cut hay on side hills that put such a bias in him that he'd have to wet himself down and nail himself to the barn to straighten out. People are afraid now. I don't like that."

He climbed out and started for the house. "If you could take all the good things you got and put them with the good things we had, this would be quite a world. But you can't do it. Good and bad get mixed up. Living ain't like shopping in a general store."

That night he sang songs in imitation of Lawrence Hill. He told stories about bears stealing stoves from trappers' cabins and being tracked to caves where the bears had the stoves set up and were making pea soup.

"That's another thing," I remarked, as I started for bed. "People don't tell stories any more."

Alanson wouldn't be pinned down. "We only told them because we didn't have any magazines."

The next day was brilliant in the fall sun. We went out into the big river bottom field, and Alanson knelt and worked his hands down into the loam to the limit of his reach. He came up with a handful of black earth, fragrant, loose, and promising.

"As good a land as lays outdoors," he said. "About thirty years ago, I pulled the last stump from this field. It was a big stump and it had always bothered the plow. I ripped it loose. I thought to myself that that was the last stump there'd ever be on the fields of this farm."

I stood quietly. Alanson looked up and then he scanned the field which was spotted with knee-high spruces and pines. We both knew that in a few years the far side of the farm would be hidden from the road.

"It's all right," he said. "The trees will hold the soil. Some day they'll need this land again. The land can wait."

"Alanson," I said, "I can't. . . . "

"Never mind," he said. "You got land of your own. I know that. You ain't going to plow this field. I wasn't thinking that you should. Nobody's got to be sorry about this field. It's done its work. That's the trouble with being old. Everytime you mention anything, people think you're sorry it's gone or changed."

"You're not old, Alanson."

"I'm forty years older than I had a right to expect to live to be when I was born. I'm old enough. But these hills is older and they'll be here when I'm gone, and when you're gone. All we can do is to pass on some of the things we've learned. The hills can pass on strength. Every time it's needed they can pass it on. When it ain't needed, they can wait until it is. A man can't do that. There comes a time when he can't wait. He has to try to tell people things that they ain't ready to be told. That don't seem right, but that's the way it is."

"Well," I said, "we do the best we can."

"We do better," he said, "when our time gets shorter. That's funny too, because then we don't really have the strength to do better."

He didn't have much strength at all. He died in the spring.

We buried him in the rain, driving to the cemetery along a road brightened by fresh green leaves, spotted with the blossoms of pin cherry and old apple trees. We drove past the farms where the woods were creeping in, past the decay of the work of many men, past the winter-sagged roofs of the empty barns.

We drove past the good land in the valleys below the hills, the hills that are the strength of Maine, the hills that will always be there. ∎

Lilac Children

The lot on which was placed this mildewed mansion is living ledge, solid granite, sloping toward the bay. Soil has been added by nature and by man, but the soil is thin.

When we came here there was a lush lilac, growing in a pocket. It is an old lilac, planted half a century ago at least, as a root sprout taken from a parent which was blooming when the Civil War began.

The big lilac seems to have been well tended and it was well placed. But twenty feet or so away, there is another lilac, I think almost as old, that somehow managed to hold on to life with soil so scant that nowhere can a bar be thrust more than six inches deep. It has nourished itself with what its roots could wrest from the granite.

When I first saw the giant lilac in bloom, I admired it, of course. It blooms gloriously. It hides its trunks and leaves with purple masses.

The little lilac, though, has more appeal to me. It had my pledge of help from the time I noted its stunted foliage and dwarfed flowers. It looked as though it had almost decided to give up. It looked tired.

I spoke to it. I believe in speaking to those things with which I hope to have a friendship. I speak to cars, always, when they join the family. I speak to tractors and saws and trees. Who is certain where there is, or is not, a spark of recognition?

To the lilac, I said, "You hold on. Help is coming."

We didn't have the money that would have bought a balanced health ration in a bag. All we had was willingness and admiration.

I dug the turf away from the lilac's base, thinking to remove the competition for nourishment and moisture. But the roots were just below the turf and I had to run across the road and steal some soil where soil was not too plentiful but where it seemed that some small portion could be spared.

Every day, beside that lilac, I buried shredded garbage. In the fall I gave the bush a limited quantity of gathered leaves and in the spring I added nitrogen.

The lilac seemed beyond responding. The other shrubs we worked with, the quince, syringa, weigela, and honeysuckle, stretched and spread and took on firmer muscle tone. The mountain ash, the cedars, and the spruces had to be discouraged with the snips from growing much too fast in gratitude.

But lethargy possessed that lilac. The next spring there were two leafless segments. In June, I sawed them off, noting that another one was barely living.

I found some old manure that year and heaped it in a mound around my friend. We pruned. We watered. One day, in desperation, I buried half my noontime sandwich near one root.

I said to it, "Listen, you have to make some effort. Half the secret of life is the desire to defy death."

But it didn't look defiant. It looked resigned.

The next spring, another section was dead. I had some tree fertilizer. I punched holes as deeply as I could and filled them with this chemical of richness. We tried something else, too. We left the new whips that sprouted from the bottom of the trunk.

That last was the key. The new whips grew to amazing size by autumn. The next year, two more old branches failed to show life but the whips branched out and one of them bloomed.

There are only a few gnarled tough old branches now. They are hanging on, I'm sure, just to help protect the thrifty new sprouts from too much exposure. Their leaves are smaller than ever. Their bloom will be a token, not a display.

But the bush will be more lush than it has been since we came. There is a lesson in that. I'm not sure what it is, but it is there. It might be from Tennyson ... "The old order changeth, yielding place to new."

The healthy, thriving, big lilac near the road shades out its offspring. It still wants prominence. But it doesn't spread as fast as does the new growth from the bush which was content to leave the stage to its thrifty children.

I'll have to think on that when I get time.   ■

Smell of Early Summer

The summer heat is promising its presence. It has been long enough on its way. It seems likely to make up in intensity for its lateness, so I'll accept that offer to make amends.

As I sit here, I am immersed, to the fullest possible capability of absorption, in odors which any manufacturer would give huge royalties to be able to duplicate. I am immersed in Maine.

The wind is off the sea, not a great wind, only a wind of salt dampness, dampness tainted with faint smoke from somebody's driftwood fire. The fire must be on the rock beach. I could see it from the upper windows if I looked, but I am not going to be an invader of privacy. That would be a poor reward for the provider of that hint of smoke that mixes with the sea.

This is the season of life. This is the season of smells. This is the heat banked, dew forming, dirt steaming, period of growth and fresh sensations. This is early summer in Maine. It came late, but it is early summer.

I have cut the grass and the sun has partially cured the clippings. The lilac has reached full bloom. The purple is a heavy mass, but the perfume-stronger white is thinner this year. The French Lilac, a heathen pretender, is blossom loaded, too, but it has almost no smell at all. I have no real love for it. It is pretty, but it is never pervading.

The crab apple tree is solid with blossoms. The odor haunts.

From across the bay I smell the horse chestnut and its honey locust companion. The blend is beautiful.

I cut the grass in my bare feet. It was damp and gloriously cool where I stepped. I trimmed the cedars and the firs, restricting their growth to preserve the view. So some of the smells are crushed tips and snipped blades.

The sun is going down and the bare ledge is blending with the mossy fringe. I can see now that the lupin is budded, not ready to bloom at all, but budded. Down by the bay lie four cherry whips that I condemned because they were competing with a mountain ash that I pamper.

"Mountain Ash" ... Aunt Eva says, "Roundwood," and my mother says, "Rowan," but whatever the name, the berries grow red in the fall and lure the robins as the robins gather to go south.

When I was twelve years old, I shot the head off a partridge as he sat in a mountain ash tree. I shot it off with a .22 rifle. Afterwards, saddened by the limp bundle that had been bird, by the red which was not berries, I was sorry too late. Most sorrow comes too late.

I do not shoot partridges any more, or squirrels, or deer. I do not have a fetish about it. I simply prefer not to do it. A psychiatrist might make something of that, but if he did, he would have to consider also the blood of those who would have been glad to see another spring ... the spring of peace.

That thought intruded. I did not mean for it to intrude. The cherry whips came to mind because there seems to be a bit of the acrid cherry in this solid bank of smells that closes ever closer in.

I sit here and smell summer and wish for descriptive words, but in the end I cannot even sit. I get up and reach out to grasp the blend that cannot be grasped. Like youth and lyric love and everything most precious, the smells cannot be hoarded or postponed. Postponement brings absolute loss.

It seems to me, sometimes, that I have lived always within reach of blended scents and possible loves that I allowed to slip away, too little savored.

Sweet fern at the edge of the woods, crushed by the horses as the logs gouged the dirt; woodsmoke and hot iron in a farmhouse kitchen; balsam blisters, broken by young thumbs; peeled bark from pines, browning in June sun; summer sawdust, pine sweet, oak sour, hemlock antiseptic though fester bringing; black birch slabs from the saw; inner bark from yellow birch, mint reminiscent; checkerberries, wintergreen, aspen flowers; pitch pine and cedar shavings.

Anyone could name more. They were all gifts, just as the soft lips above the gardenia corsage were offered as a gift.

Too much long gone . . . no more. I'm going to absorb sweet summer in Maine . . . today, and tomorrow, and tomorrow. ■

Ridge Runner's Lament

This river doesn't sing. It's a pretty river, I suppose, and people who like the ocean like the junction of waters, the throb of the tide pressing and the river flowing and the resultant psychological feeling that change comes slowly.

This land doesn't shelter. This land stretches in flatness. People who like the idea of standing in the wind and letting the mist-spray from the waves hit their cheeks while they look out into greyness ... those people like this land. They like the beaches and the level ground and the early sun and the late sun. This land gets both.

This is a beautiful country and people come from miles away to look at it and tell themselves that it's beautiful. I don't deny beauty when I say that flat country just doesn't appeal to me. Neither does a river that keeps trying but can't ever make a complete change.

There are probably traces of water in this river that have been touched by other traces of water that have never quite made it to the sea. Some of those drops of water may have been trying for fifty years. They get to the river mouth and the tide pushes them back.

I'm tired of a tidal river because to me it is foreign. I want a river that moves. I'm tired of flatness. I want ridges and hills and the sudden sunsets that spread glory in back of the hardwoods and turn the spruces black. I want mountains behind the ridges. I don't want high mountains that crowd. I want low mountains

14

with rock cliffs, mountains just high enough to show white in early October and warn me of what is going to come.

I wouldn't deny the beauty of the sea. I wouldn't deny the love that the coastal dweller feels for the spray and the smell of salt hay and the nearness of the wide water that can be a road to almost any place on earth.

But a man has a right to choose. And this river doesn't sing. This river is slow and its bed is clay and sand and silt. This river has no boulders that make tuned noises in the night. I want a river that changes every hour. I want a river that rushes. I want a river where I can kneel and drink and know that the place my lips touched is ten feet downstream by the time I have swallowed.

I want a river that flows free. I want a river that flows through my heart.

It's crowded down here. The houses are close. The hammers pound every day and bring the houses closer. The area boosters look for more people, more people, more people. People are progress. People are prosperity. People are wonderful.

That's all right. I can stand people. But I don't like their permanent presence in planned proximity. I like to be with them and then I like to be alone. When I'm alone, I don't want to know that there is a house fifty feet away in which lives another man who also wants to be alone.

So I'm going up the river and build myself a house, just a little house. Then I can live a week here and a week there. I'm going to build my house by the water where the water sings. I'm going to build it in the spruces and the firs where the smell comes through the window cracks.

I'm going to have a cedar grove where I can rip a handful of fragrance as I come and go, fragrance to rub between my palms so I can spread fresh smelling stains on the front of my shirt.

That way, the rest of the family can have the sea and I can have the little spring that boils sand from its clear bottom and draws the mineral strength from the middle of the earth.

They can have the sun on the sand and I can have the shadow of the pasture pine, tolerated in its limby growth because of the needles it spreads on its southern side to make an early spring softness when the snow is still in the fields and the deeper woods.

I don't want my mountain house only for the summer. I want it for the winter, too, when the wind blows and seals the fire and me into a nest of silence that allows thought.

Because a man needs people but there comes a time when he needs himself as well.   ■

The Presence of the Past

When men left the hill farms, the woods came in, but the woods were erratic in the taking back of the cleared land. For the most part, the advance was gradual from the ridge downward, but there were also leaps.

There is still a strip of pasture, ever narrowing, parallel to the slope. Below the pasture, the trees press the backyard fence lines of the few remaining houses, kept by sporadic cutting from taking over the last hundred feet to the edge of the road.

Above the pasture, the woods are in possession, accepting the apple trees as kin, circling the lilacs because the lilacs have power to protect their territory and smother stray seeds.

Some men, when they walk, would rather walk the deep woods, harvested or untouched, either one, but never cleared or planned for anything but timber growth. I walk those woods at times because there is a satisfaction in knowing that there are twenty or thirty or fifty miles of woods beyond and that a man could press into them until he became a part of them in fact as well as in thought.

Usually, though, I would rather walk the acres where men lived and used the land for pasture or for field crops long ago.

There are thousands of these acres in the hills of the upper river. Some were the sites of old buildings. Some were back fields. Some were orchards and some were providers of extra hay, marked by the decayed timbers of old barns, once filled in summer and emptied in deep winter when their contents could most easily be transferred to the barns at home.

17

It is the finding of the old foundations and the tracing of the once plain barnyard borders that I enjoy. Wherever men worked, they left something. It isn't physical, but it takes the physical remnants to recreate it.

When a man walks through a region like that, he can feel the presence of his predecessors. That isn't truly mystic. It doesn't take any great sensitivity to be affected. The difference between men and animals of lesser intellect may be proved by the fact that men press something into the land they work and use. Other animals do not.

Oh, if a bear has been roaming a region and is still in undefined residence, there is an odor and there are marks and a man can sense the being of the bear and so may walk warily, not really fearing the bear but respecting the bear's right not to be startled or surprised into acting with unplanned belligerence.

But that is only when the bear is in presence or lately gone. A week or so, at most, will clear the air and free the land from the bear's imprint.

An old settler is not that easily removed. He made more enduring marks and that is not surprising. He tried to.

Here is a field where he mowed. There are the boulders that shortened sections of his swath on the first pass down the eastern edge and on the third pass down the southern edge.

There is the rotted stump of the huge pine which he crossed his pasture line to cut because it was thirty inches on the butt and limbless, probably, for the first hundred feet, topped only by a tuft that brought it nourishment, somehow, but was easily removed after the last log was marked for bucking.

The pine served a double purpose. Its stump was a shaded seat, used more often as the mower aged, until finally either the stump or the mower aged too much, and that was that.

The walker knows all this. Somewhere in town there may be someone left who could tell him if he asked, but he doesn't need to ask. He knows. He can feel it and he can see it if he knows what to look for.

Part of the sadness of the new forests is that so few do know what to look for. Many hunters are superb woodsmen but, when they sense the men who worked the land they walk, they are only conscious of something and that something is undefined. When they come to a stone wall, they know that there was much labor in its building but they cannot taste the sweat that came each spring as the new stones were barred and lifted.

When they see a mid-field pile of stone, they don't know that buried underneath it there's a boulder too big to move and so, resignedly, covered by the frost thrust crop and used thus to shorten the trip to the edge of the field.

On all the old lands, there are lessons. They are the marks men made, the intimacies of an era. They should not be lost.

■

True Heritage

I remember the spring on the hill farm, the farm of the drain-
ing instead of the gift. It was only forty acres, that farm, and
half of it was scrawny second growth woodlot spotted with
decrepit maples which did the best they could but produced
sap that needed a hundred gallons to boil down to a gallon of
seven pound syrup.

There was nothing left in the soil but the remnants of effort.
The fields dried out overnight because the gravel was thin
inches from the wind that whipped the topsoil. There was a
ten acre pasture that grew a half inch of moss covering, broken
here and there by some particularly vigorous bunch of tough
grass. There was a juniper beside every rock and that meant
there were a lot of junipers.

The ploughed fields were almost as feeble as the pasture.
They could start a crop but the growth was as strained as the
effort of a ten year old to chin himself for the seventh time. A
man could stand in those fields and hear the sound of the
straining. The corn tasselled in August exhaustion, saving its
last thrust for the filling of the ears. Even the turnips were limp
and wormy and fiber crossed before they were the size of
crabapples and so judged worth pulling up.

But I remember the spring on the hill farm because in the
spring, for just awhile, it was green. And I think it had a memory
of green pasts. I think it must have known that it was old, old,
old, and worn, worn, worn, but that it had once been part of a
newness which promised and produced but found that it had
given more than the owner deserved.

I moved onto that farm in the winter. The spring showed the neglect that the snow had hidden. I was just settling into that section that year. I had a mill to set up and some trading to do and some stone to haul and the summer went into fall while I was still unable to do much except plant the weary garden that tried again and failed again and then browned over and prepared for the winter when it could at least rest.

But that was the winter I gave that farm a little hope. That was the winter I hauled sawdust and manure after dark and spread it deeply with a dump truck. I cleaned out the scrub growth from the woods and I brought back a load of sawdust to scatter every time I took out a load of firewood. I hauled old chicken manure from abandoned henhouses and dumped it in piles wherever I could get a truck between the trees. I put the lime to the pasture on top of the snow and I put sawdust on the pasture, too. Sawdust was cheap. It was as cheap as labor.

I sold the place the next fall. My work kept moving further away. But I had the reward of one more spring and I saw that field stay green through the manure all summer long.

I don't know what happened to the land after I left. But I do know that I gave it a little something to compensate for what it had given for so long and tried to give for even longer. A man ought to try to do that once in awhile, especially a man who hasn't ever done much else that will have any permanent value.

It was years after I sold the hill farm that I was talking to Alanson Hunnewell. Alanson was discussing crops and soil and men.

He said, "When I was a boy, even then, people were talking about worn out land. But they didn't know anything much to do for it except move away. Farmers know better now, and that's good. A man ought to do something for the land when the land has done so much for him."

I remember him saying that and he said it with all the sincerity that a man could say anything. And I agree with him. If I ever had time enough and money to use, I'd take another piece of land and do what I tried to do with the hill farm, except I'd finish the job. I'd put it right back where it originally was.

Because the land is the only true heritage there is. ∎

Maine Is in My Heart: Cedar River

When the sun comes to Cedar River, it comes over the ridges to the east and it seems happy to be back for another day. When the sun sets, it tears itself to shreds in its disappointment. It casts colored glory across the tops of the trees. Then it retires and sulks its way around the rest of the world while it makes itself presentable for one more gift of its gleam to Cedar River.

Just before the light fades, the outlines of Deer Mountain become distinct, clean, and stern, a reminder that much rock must crumble before the earth is destroyed. This is a solace to the Cedar River people. They seldom look, they seldom observe, but they know that the mountain is there, and the mountain is a comfort. The shadows it casts are caves of retreat.

There is a solace also in the river flow. The river moves, yet the river stays. It is there, but it has passed. A man cannot step into the same river twice. The man changes and the river changes. Only change is constant. Change is eternal. Thus change differs from Cedar River, for Cedar River comes and goes. The years of its being are vague and its presence is uncertain.

Cedar River people have always been more undecided than Hamlet about whether to be or not to be. Their ancestors built them a town in a hidden land that was mostly gravel and river and ledges and ridges and hills. Sometimes the people grow weary of the need to force growth from seeds sown on a rock,

22

and they retreat from reality. Thus they are not there when the census taker comes and their town torments the topographers.

But, usually, strangers who penetrate the ridge-clinging clouds are permitted to see what they are capable of seeing. Surprisingly, some strangers earn themselves a place in heaven by refusing to go back downriver and announce that they have discovered the origins of fantasy. They see, but they stay silent. They deserve the bliss of the blessed.

Other strangers, however, look at the froth instead of the ferment. They leave town quickly, fearful of being contaminated by the obvious stupidity, backwardness, and scorned simplicity. They never find Cedar River again, but they use the name of the village as a reference in some related travelogue, probably as the location of an adventure which is a big lie.

These people are more lied to than lying. The biggest lie of all is the lie that the surface of Cedar River tells such scorners. Because Cedar River, of course, has no simplicity. Simplicity is the one thing it never had. Simplicity cannot live with vagueness. Simplicity must be bounded.

And the boundaries of Cedar River are undefined. The woods intrude on the settlement and the settlement intrudes on the woods. Sometimes a man will go to his hayfield and find that the spruces have sprouted since the last cutting. Sometimes the deer will seek out a beech grove and find that someone has taken fifty or sixty thousand feet of logs and a winter's warmth, and the slash lies scattered.

Neither change is really a hardship. Hay gets increasingly unwanted as the tractors roar. There are other beeches and the beech trash will rot quickly, fast rot being a characteristic of beeches. Big bursting raspberries and tender hardwood sprouts will fill the cutover grove in a few years, feeding deer and bears and providing raspberry pies.

It may be the mingling of men and the wild things along the vague lines which separate the natural from the semi-controlled that has kept the Cedar River people from conforming to the patterned lives of the down river world.

Patterns are possible where a factory is a factory and an office is an office, hot in summer, cooler in winter, but an entity of sameness, in the same place, with the same contours.

But patterns become distorted where a different trail leads every season into a different woods and where even the purpose of the trail changes with the weather and the wind.

In the winter, the snow stretches on each side of the trampled route. In the spring, that route is forbidden because of the freshets and the swamps, but the diversion is among new flowers and the smell of growth. In the fall, there may be no trail at all, but only a wary walking and watching for fallen branches that will crack and warn the quarry.

In the winter the cold is a stimulant in the morning and a challenging enemy at night. In the summer the heat floats with the smell of sunbaked downed timber, a separate smell for each species. The spring woods are friendly with fragrance of a headier kind. In the fall the sun grows more valuable and there is a sense of coming quietness.

So time has so many divisions that only two are important. There is daylight which permits certain activities. There is darkness which encourages others. Both are needful and both can be enjoyed. Years as years mean nothing. Years are relative. They are remembered only by events, and those events local.

Last Sunday was long ago and forty years ago was the day before yesterday. This confuses visitors because it confuses chronology. Cedar River doesn't care. By next week, Cedar River may have decided not to exist, but in a month it may change its mind.

Thus all that counts is what happened within the interest circle of the town. Dates are numbers to be written in a book and the book put away.

What matters is that Thomas Webster came home two years before Andy Parsons, stung by a trading defeat, took physical work with my uncle Tom, and got hemlock festered and died. That was the same year that Randy Gage hung himself, and it was just after that year that Uncle Oscar set his underwear on fire, and that was about six months or six weeks or six days after Zeke Benson tried to fly off the barn roof. Uncle Jake got the frogs in his stomach about two years later, because Doc Yates was the first one to tell about Susan going to church with the mice in her hat.

And all these things depended on each other and yet none of them had any relationship except the relationship of time and town, and neither time nor town had any real meaning or importance except in casual talk while the men whittled gouges out of the Post Office steps.

"Do you remember when Tom Rogers shot Brent Moore?"

"I was thinking about the Caruthers' windmill."

"When was that?"

"Seems as though it was the fall after the Square Eddy jam."

"It was before that. I'll tell you when it was. When was the fire in the hotel garage?"

"I don't know. They were logging at Burnt Creek—that's how I remember that."

"Well, then, it was the same summer we skidded Minnie."

"No, No, No, No."

Memories are not neat like an orderly classroom full of Mrs. Kelly's scholars. Memories are jumbled in a bureau drawer with a covering of folded handkerchiefs, placed just so, in order that a burglar looking for money will know that the housewife is tidy.

Impressions of a burglar are important.

Defiance of logic, yet with a logic that is local; realization that error is the usual result of effort and that results may be cause-less or controlled by the unseen; scoffing at superstition that returns in the night, acceptance of moods; those are the charac-teristics of Cedar River, disorganized in its being, capricious in its existence, unconcerned with its chances for glory.

Glory is winged and so are angels. Neither could land in the river grove. Yet both would be helped down off the mountain and given a room for the night and referred to in the same terms as a kind stranger who promised not to tell where he had been.

The room would have modern plumbing, the mark of Wilmer Hobber. Wilmer came to Cedar River twenty years ago, or maybe

thirty years ago, or maybe ten years ago. He came the year after
Cousin Susan married the short order cook who was married
many times already. That was the same year that my cousin
Paul ran across the field in hunting season with a pair of antlers
tied to his head. Not one of the city hunters shot at Paul, and
Paul collected seven bets in marbles, jack-knives, and fish
hooks.

He also collected a few welt-raising wallops from Uncle Waldron, who tempted fate all the time but believed he was unique
in the alacrity of his avoidance.

Later that same day, two sheep were sacrificed on the hillside
and brought into town on a Detroit built altar, four hunters
claiming them as Caribou and two insisting that they were
musk oxen. The Canadian Club advertising agency did not welcome the heroes with cameras and a bolstering beverage,
which was just as well because they had visited my uncle Oscar
the evening before and had been bolstered to their bottoms.

One of the hunters had a hole in his hat.

The fine was one hundred dollars. That was a small sum
compared to the price the glum group later paid Deak Trembley
for the sheep. The sheep would have been startled had they
been able to hear the recitation of their virtues and their pedi-
grees, being accustomed to being addressed by their owner as,
"stupid, stubborn, cross-eyed, mongrel bastards."

Glory to the guns. Mighty is their range and varied are their
targets and startling is the bzzt of their bullets past the ears of
the loggers.

And glory to Wilmer Hobber, the prophet of plumbing, even
though Wilmer vulgarized our language. People now speak
casually of going to the toilet. In gentler times, folks used
"Facilities."

Wilmer changed that. I'm glad he did.

I was downriver awhile back and a man spoke jeeringly of
conservative notions, bred in a conservative economy. He
spoke in favor of progress, which I consider mostly a problem.
He said he didn't want to go back. He was in love with

his washer, his drier, his conditioner of air, his mixer and his muddler and his spongy synthetic softness, wall to wall, immune to sinful stains except for the unavoidable piddling of his Pekingese.

"Years ago," he said, "people had iceboxes with big pans under them and the pans had to be emptied or else the water ran out on the floor. Think of the inconvenience of that. I didn't like my grandfather's farm. . . . I didn't like . . . I didn't like . . . "

I didn't like him. I suspected his grandfather's farm didn't like him, either. I wondered if he had tried to find that farm lately. Farms have a way of disappearing in the growing pines when there is no caretaker left for whom they care.

But I sat quietly and I thought of the inconvenience of an icebox. I sat quietly . . . quietly . . . for there was no urge in me to be singled out for sarcasm. The inconvenience of an icebox . . . yes . . . inconvenience . . . yes.

The ice was heavy and the sawdust stuck. The lift was high and the cakes were slippery and my front teeth went when the tongs slipped. My father bought me a bridge, but the abutments wore out. My partial plate flew to the timekeeper's lap, during my oratorical outburst in a school debate. Mrs. Kelly clobbered me because she said that Cranston would never have been given the decision if the bicuspids hadn't bounced.

She said, "Had I wanted a comedian to defend the Volstead Act, I would have picked Casimer and let him tell his story of Pat and the apple pie."

But an icehouse was a lovely place to play, for young and old. It was cool and dark and the sawdust was dry on top. The eight and ten year olds could rest and hide in the acrid dimness at any time of day, but in the evenings the sixteen year olds and their giggling girl friends insisted on solitude, not being interested in the comments of the young.

The source of the ice was a setting for romance. Even the icebox was better than the pundit's picture. We didn't have any pan to empty. My father drilled a hole in the floor.

I couldn't tell that to the mocking modernist. He would have said, "Why didn't your cellar fill up with water?" We didn't have a cellar. I couldn't have said that either. He would have said, "With no cellar, why didn't your plumbing freeze?"

Bless the logical. It exposes flaws. We didn't have any cellar and our plumbing didn't freeze because we had no plumbing.

Bless Wilmer Hobber who came at some unknown time with a truckload of fixtures, bought when the Cranston Commercial House was torn down. There is a mark on time. There is a definiteness. The Commercial House was torn down twenty years after it was modernized and it was modernized just eighteen years before my cousin Paul bought the hardware store and started charging folks for things they hadn't bought. That should date Wilmer's coming to the satisfaction of any historian.

The Commercial House fixtures were well preserved. Wilmer brought us corner lavatories and hopper toilets and bathtubs on claw cast feet. Deak Trembley didn't want a bathroom but he bought a lavatory, anyway. He said it was just the thing for a horse trough in his box stall. It was perfect for four years until a new horse ate the stopper, which suddenly stopped the horse.

But most of the plumbing served better than that. It was at least an improvement, I suppose, over facilities.

Our facilities at home were at the back of the woodshed and the woodshed broke a forty acre stretch of field where the wind was unimpeded. Anyone who used the facilities brought in an armful of wood. Wood was the excuse. The need for wood justified the visit, removing the need to state the purpose.

But the wind blew hard across the field and Cedar River comment sometimes forgot the dainty in deference to jokes.

If the kitchen were full of people and a lightly built woman looked and said, "I think you need some more wood," and rose to go, some happy man in tune with nature would reply, "I beg your pardon, please, but that wind is blowing strong and if I were you, I'd pick up the wood FIRST."

Harsh was the humor, uncaring of convention. The earth seemed always close, and seems close still. The dust of the ground filters down into the tops of boots and the stains of the soil are often the forerunners of procreation. Nature marks her own. Even the stories concur.

And the stories breed belief. A man who lives in Cedar River is not easily startled by tales from the outside. He believes as he expects belief. Thus he is called gullible.

Cedar River believes stories about shrewd traders because Andy Parsons lived in Cedar River, and Andy could start down the road any old morning with a handful of turnip seed and end up in town with two crates of eggs and a spring lamb.

Uncle Oscar could arrive similarly laden, but Uncle Oscar wouldn't have been trading. Uncle Oscar would have been finding things where they weren't lost.

The story of the man who built a boat in the cellar would have seemed like idle tea-gossip to Cedar River, because Joe Caruthers once put a mail order manure spreader together in his living room and everyone in town made a suggestion about the next step. Joe's solution was the simplest one offered. He ran the wagon tongue out the window and hooked a skidding team to it and pulled the whole business right on through the side of the house, spreading lath, splinters, and plaster for fifty feet.

There was a fringe benefit. Joe got some lime in his garden.

Outsiders misunderstand. The hired comedian at the Ladies' Aid Benefit show told about a farmer who hung a tuning fork beside his cow a month before calving time and got a heifer that bawled in true "G."

Nobody laughed. Everybody believed it. After all, Jonas P. Hall played the violin to his kitten every night, and when the kitten turned into a cat and went courting, he had his pick of the fence felines because he could sit on the roof of the woodshed and work his way through the whole chorus of "Ramona."

Exaggeration must be a comparative. A town must be what its people are or what they would have been had they chosen to exist at the time when the observations were made. A town must be people and memories. That's what Cedar River is. That's what Lieutenant Jenks understood and what Lyman never would be capable of learning.

People, that's what Cedar River displays and shields, Gages and Caruthers, Jenkins, Reynolds, Halls—Fishbait Olson—Uncle Jake—men who wish and men who work and men who just don't give a damn—women, longing sometimes for romance, and sometimes shucking off the offered need.

Uncle Oscar's still, provider of too potent bliss, is gone. It went with drama stern enough to interest Hollywood except that Hollywood believes that nothing really worthy of its time takes place, or ever did, across a line just east of Kansas.

Andy Caruthers and I smashed the still with an axe. We knew that what we did was good and yet we lingered. We only put poor Uncle Oscar brewing batches in a crock, mild potions made of old potato skins and prunes and yeast and peaches. We didn't stop the message . . . the hint for health for all.

"If I was you, I'd just remember it's the bugs that brings diseases on. Don't never drink unless you're sure that what you're drinking will kill bugs."

That's Uncle Oscar speaking. He takes his own advice.

Cedar River doesn't worry. That may be the only thing a viewer needs to see. That may explain emergence and retreat.

The outside world fears war and lack of hygiene. The outside world fears psycho signs and sudden death.

Cedar River speaks of war, but war is vague.

"What the Hell? We had some wars before. We sent our men and most come back. We got a monument beside the river."

The quoted man is Jesse Hill. He went to war in nineteen seventeen. He now confuses war with American Legion Conventions at Atlantic City. He dreads the thought of both, but he went once and he would go again. He says Atlantic City is more deadly.

Hygiene is a word. Mrs. Kelly once was told by some Augusta dope to teach hygiene. She wouldn't do it. But Cedar River in a casual way can view its innards on a lighted screen, night after night, and not be worried by the terrible effects of not rubbing, rolling, or spraying. Cedar River doesn't give a hearty damn just how a statue smells or what a man should use to shave a peach.

And psycho-swash, the hell with that. Nobody in town ever got worried and paid a man a hundred dollars to find out that all his troubles came from childhood viewing of a fly caught in a spider web; a nasty, dirty fly when flying, but, when caught, a pitiable victim of an indecent ogre.

In Cedar River, kids on rainy days get bounties for the flies they swat inside the kitchen, spiders too. I don't know what the scale is now. It used to be a hundred for a cent, a hundred flies, that is. A spider brought a little more, but brought some hazards, too, for when a spider's smashed, it rains.

How dry are the fields?

Oh, Hell, it may not be the lack of worry. It may be because there's no routine. Every hour of every day is new. Maybe nothing happens more dramatic than the trees put on an hour's growth. Maybe Freddie Grouper falls through spring-shot ice because he tries to fish too close to breakup time.

If Freddie does—and Freddie DID—the word gets carried upstreet to the general store. No speed seems needed. People know that Freddie's going to cling or swim or else he's going to sink. It's up to Freddie for awhile. Freddie was the one who wanted pike or perch. The town needs time. There has to be a brief debate about whose ladder is the longest and the best to shove out on the ice so Freddie can catch hold. After a long winter in his woolies, it's just as well for Freddie to soak awhile. Otherwise he'll be obnoxious while he's drying out. He'll SMELL.

Hang on, Freddie, hang on, while the river washes away your sins of omission. You didn't spray or rub or roll. You smell like Freddie. You smell like four months sewed tight, protected and pore clogged. Hang on, you smelly bastard.

That time, Freddie got out. The town saved him. They marched him down to the store and they peeled him and they rubbed him with old grain sacks and they gave him the dregs of a quart that Uncle Oscar had persuaded Clint Reynolds to buy for the sake of humanity, and to share for the sake of the nerves of the worriers about Freddie.

But more quarts were produced and after Freddie had gagged on his portion, and after the town had given him a few oral ideas about how stupid he was and how stupid his ancestors had been and how stupid his children would undoubtedly be, they all had a long drink in relief.

Then they all had another drink. They settled in and they drank for the rest of the day because their mittens were wet anyway and they had just saved a man from an icy grave and if that didn't deserve a drink, nothing ever did deserve a drink.

Freddie's rescue was only temporary. He drowned later. He drowned in the old quarry pit, looking for scrap iron that wasn't there. When he fell in the river he didn't drown, because folks on the bank could see him and hear him. In the quarry pit, he drowned because he was down there all alone.

One time he didn't, one time he did.

The town got drunk both times. Either result called for a drink. "Here's to Freddie."

Give him hell when you save him. List his virtues when you can't. Take a drink anyway, for effort made or unmade.

Either way, "Here's to Freddie."

I grew up with Freddie. I liked him. He was good in Geography. He was good in a fight. He had courage. He had too much courage. When I got pocketed by four Gages and one of them hit me in the back with a baseball bat, it was Freddie who jumped in and helped. We still took a beating, but it wasn't so lonesome.

Freddie was probably lonesome for a few seconds in that quarry pit, but thinking of that doesn't help a man sleep.

Silently, then, here's to Freddie.

And here's to the complexity that will always confute the shallow understanding of the man who muddles somehow through the haze, and stops his car, and stands on Mr. Turner's store steps, and drinks a charge of fizzy fluff and says, "God, what a graveyard. God, what a backwoods hole. I wonder what keeps them awake. I wonder if they hibernate in winter."

You hammerhead, they hibernate at will.

Symbolic smugness, stupid status-seeking snobbery, stands right where Jonas Hall once stopped a war with poetry.

Beside the stranger stands Agnes Slade. She doesn't hear him say, "Bunch of God Damned vegetables. A herd of cows has got more feelings."

She doesn't even see him. She hasn't seen much for a long, long time. She lives with Robbie Morton and Robbie Morton doesn't live in Cedar River any more. Robbie doesn't live anywhere. Robbie had a fault. He couldn't believe.

Robbie Morton knew but he didn't believe. That was Robbie's trouble. He knew. He knew as surely as he knew that the mountain core was rock, that the Square Eddy spring was sweet, that the night valley mist in August would evaporate with the sun.

He knew that he was the beloved of Agnes Slade. But he couldn't believe in the truth of this knowledge. He denied what he knew.

For Agnes Slade was the cause of the morning song of the birds. It was for Agnes Slade that they left their nests and sang. Only a fool thought differently.

It was for Agnes Slade that the moon glowed full and bright. Agnes Slade called the moon and the moon came up. It was for Agnes Slade that the little streams tried so hard to rush down the rocks to add their volume to the roar of the river in the gorges.

And Robbie Morton's solid realism denied the possibility that his dream of love was not a dream, but a fact; that Agnes Slade loved as she was loved; that she loved him. She had told him that she loved him. She had looked with love and acted with love. So he knew there was love. But he didn't believe.

A blither man would have accepted the proofs of his senses and accepted, consequently, the truth. A more casual man would not even have thought of doubting, would have enjoyed even the presence of pretense.

But Robbie's need was so great, his desire was so intense, his love was so complete, that acceptance of proof was impossible. His entire life had been a saga of disappointment. He had never quite been able to do what he wanted to do. When he succeeded, he succeeded only in part. He knew that he had nothing to offer Agnes Slade that could not be exceeded by some other man.

He saw Agnes three evenings a week. At each meeting he was lifted and exalted and elated and happy. Every touch was a message, every kiss was a pledge. When he left Agnes at her father's door, he was dreamy with a light headed glory. He knew he was loved.

About two hours later, he tossed in bed and he started to doubt. By morning, his doubt was full. By noon, doubt was gone and disbelief had taken control. That was the sequence of Robbie's days.

The end was inevitable. Nobody can reassure forever, even one who understands. There came a night when Agnes said, "If you don't believe me—if you can't believe me—go away. All right. I don't mean what I say. All right. I'm lying to you. So go away. Don't come here anymore."

Robbie went away. By morning he was convinced that he had been right all along, that Agnes did not care, that he would be lonely forever.

He took a rifle and he put a bullet in his head. As he pulled the trigger, he took one more blow from fate. He realized that he was a fool. His knowledge of love became belief. But he was too late. He never even heard the roar or smelled the smoke in the quiet kitchen.

Agnes Slade never married. She lived for forty years alone. She lived with the memory of the fact that she had broken—that she had become too tired of a hopeless task to work toward hope.

But there had never been a chance in the world that she could do anything else. A man who is determined to succeed will not necessarily succeed. But a man who is determined to be defeated will almost always get his wish. Any man can destroy himself if he is bent on such destruction. And Robbie was.

Here's to the Cedar River simplicity that doesn't exist. Here's to Freddie Grouper. Here's to Agnes Slade. Here's to Robbie Morton. Here's to the complexity I found when I was very young.

It was a winter night and I was ten years old. My friend sat by the parlor window as the road grew dark. The great limbed oaks were outlined against the snow. In the summer, those oaks were friendly, but in the winter, their shadows shifted and their shapes changed.

My friend seemed one with the oaks. Her voice was a song but it brought shivers in reaching waves. She said nothing but still she spoke. She shared with me a moment that took no time.

Reality went up the road, outside the reach of the mood. Joe Hanrahan slogged along behind his big skidding team, the loosely looped trace chains clinking link on link as the unguided horses raised their heads every few steps, distrusting the night, looking for the bend by the big maple from which they would be able to see the stable with its hay and grain and warmth.

When they came opposite our house, one horse whinnied and the other lifted his head and whinnied, too. They shook their heads and telegraphed a message of unrest along the harness. They broke into a trot, snapping the slack out of the reins, bringing Joe into a shuffling run as he threw back his weight and tried to slow them to their broken pattern. But they were still trotting when we lost their sound.

"YOU did that," I said.

I think she laughed. Then the outside shadows blended into one shadowed whole and there was no light in the room at all. There was only a heavy greyness, which denied the sight of shapes and outlines, but accentuated the presence of my friend.

I walked across to her. I stood close enough to touch had there been anything to touch.

"Please go away," I said. "I was happy until you came."

She let her laughter rise, then, until I was sure there would be a clamoring for silence from the kitchen or from the rooms above.

She said, "Anybody can be happy. Unhappiness is the gift. The unhappy see what others do not see. Need and desire and demand, those are all gifts. Besides, I am nothing. In a minute I will be gone. But I will come back in the night. Because it is too late for you to turn away. You have started to look."

I snapped on the light, and the room, of course, was empty. I followed the filtered light path to the kitchen. My father stood by the stove. He had dropped something in the fire on top of the slow burning hardwood. I could see the flicker through the chinks in the top check draft. I snapped the switch and there was light in the kitchen, too.

My father turned. "Who were you talking to there in the dark?" he asked.

"The devil, I think," I said.

"Tell me," he said.

I told him. He listened. He brought me a coffee cup and he filled it for me as he filled his own. That was new because coffee was forbidden even to my sister Liz who was two years older than I. But my father smiled.

"It's all right," he said. "A man needs a cup of coffee after he's been talking with the devil."

So I sipped as I finished my story. My father kept nodding.

"Bill," he said, "it's hard for you to believe but I was ten years old myself one time. I don't remember too well, but I think that's about the time my friend started to come to me. I couldn't drive her away and I'm glad. I never did all I wanted to do. I never did and I never will. But I'm glad she made me try."

"But I don't know how to try," I told him. "I don't know why the best things are the sad things, like when you get the first spring thaw you ought to be happy, but you're not happy for some reason. You feel all funny. You keep thinking you want to get someplace and there isn't any such place. Besides, I don't want to be unhappy all my life."

"All right," he said, "be stupid. Stupid people get what they reach for, so they're happy. They never know enough to miss the things they might have had."

"I don't want to be stupid. I want to be like Uncle Oscar and Uncle Waldron and Francis Gage, and do what I want to do, and be happy."

"I'm glad you know that Oscar and Waldron aren't stupid. But, Bill, don't ever think that Oscar is really happy. Oscar's too smart to be happy. He gave up but there was a reason. Waldron isn't happy, either. And when you put Francis Gage in the same class with Oscar, you're giving Francis a little break in the stupidity scale. That doesn't matter, though. The thing that matters is that you've started to look so it's too late for you to stop."

"She said that."

"Sure. She said it to me, maybe thirty-eight years ago."

"Did you want to be unhappy?"

"You're missing a point. Unhappiness isn't a constant. Someday you'll begin to see most of what she meant. She's you, you know. She's the beginning of real thinking. She wants you to dig under the surface."

"The surface is the most fun," I said.

"Yes," he said, "and it's a delusion, too."

That was that, and that was all. I can't go back any further than that, not into the deeper things. I can go back to memories of amusement. I can't go back to structure.

When I go back too far, I'm like the stranger on the steps, looking and not seeing.

But here's to the stranger and here's to my friend who kept me from following a course that would have led to him. Here's to Cedar River where what is, never was, and what was, still is not. Here's to a pleasant picture of turnip eating torpor and hilarious stupidity and sex and savagery.

Here's to the actions of many men, and the men's fathers, and, I hope, their sons.

Freddie Grouper had no sons. Here's to his sons unborn.

In what are we pledging the toast?

In the clear water of a spring that never flowed but stayed concealed in the subsoil of the forested hills.

Here's to my Maine, which is not on the granite coast where the cold sea is a reminder that the world is bleak and death is an actuality; where live the legends of the prudent sea captains and their cautious descendants.

Here's to the Maine of more frivolity and less adequate reasons for being; my Maine, which is in the river mists.

Trees Are Human, Almost

"A philosopher could do a lot with a pitch pine," I said to Wilmer. "A pitch pine has a lot of human attributes."

We were cutting up an unmourned specimen of that species. The discriminating wind of the day before had chosen it for destruction. I was pleased about that. The wind could have hit the white pine or the spruces. It could have taken one of my two arboreal amours, the mountain ashes. It could have taken almost any tree it wanted to take because these trees grow on a rock face which is covered by about four inches of soil.

But the wind had taken the pitch pine and we were working it up into disposable remnants. A pitch pine is not an asset except as a temporary cover while something else is growing. We knocked off its rotten hearted branches. We chopped into its minute annual rings.

"How come?" asked Wilmer. "How come a pitch pine doesn't lose its lower branches in a decent fashion like a white pine? How come it maintains this deception of life? Who is it trying to fool?"

"That's what I mean," I said. "A white pine is honest. When its lower limbs die, the bark comes off. The limbs are dead, but they're sound inside. They rot from the surface. Anybody knows they're dead. And the tree writes off the dead limbs. It seals off the sockets. It faces life without them. A pitch pine won't admit that the limbs are dead. . . . "

"Yeah," said Wilmer, "so the rot from the limbs goes right into the tree."

38

"That's the social parallel, isn't it?"

"So all right. Don't spell it out for me," he said.

I'm inclined to go along with that protest. It doesn't need spelling out. Actually it was too fine a day for a sermon. Most days are. And it was only a bit of musing anyway. It led to more musing, though. I wonder if the development of trees isn't very close to the development of men, all the way around. I wonder if Joyce Kilmer wasn't aware of this closeness. I wonder if all the many men who seem to have an affinity for forests don't recognize that evolution has dealt with trees in a kindred manner to that with which it has dealt with men.

Because in trees an observer can find the racial traits and the individual idiosyncrasies that characterize men. That may sound like a forced comparison but it's fun to think about. There are the fast growth boys, the aspens, that seem to reach their destination overnight but do not have any durability to speak of. There are the solid and stolid oaks that develop so slowly but have such strength. Then there are the fine grained maples and black cherries and yellow birches, sensitive stock from which veneer can be made to cover the faults of their fellows.

There are trees which stop growing early and spend their strength giving fruit. Even in these there are some which give fruit that has value and there are some which give fruit that is almost worthless.

There are trees which grow better if they have competition. A softwood grove will have straighter and cleaner stock if it is dense. But after awhile, the strong will kill off the weak and mature in roomy glory, protecting themselves from upstart seedlings by stealing all the sun. Hardwoods like white birches, on the other hand, seem to be more tolerant. They share the strength of sun and soil if they are crowded. They all grow too tall and too slender. No few trees are selfish enough to gain strength at the expense of the others. As a result, one bad wind will topple the whole stand. Stands of pine will blow down, too, of course, but this is mostly when they have been too slow in killing the competition or after their age has sapped their strength.

We have one more obvious parallel between trees and men. When a tree has been protected by the forest from too much wind and too much sun, if the forest is cut down and that one tree left standing, it will not live. The elements will kill it unless it is young enough to be adaptable. If a tree grows in solitude, however, it can remain in solitude.

A man could write a book about this. It would be quite a book, too. If there can be sermons in stones, there is no reason why there can't be philosophy in forests. ■

Lonesome Winter

My love went out to Helen Purdie in a wave of longing and loneliness and desperation at my inability to turn back the clock. There had been a time, three years before, when there was an answer from her and a response to my smile. This day there was not, nor had there been for some time. We stood apart.

"Helen," I said, "I have a lonesome house. How long must I wait?"

She stood on the edge of the stream with the sun shining on her and on the autumn leaves behind. She had hair that matched the yellow of the turning rock maple and a red in her cheeks that blended with the oaks. She looked like a part of the wildness and I loved her.

"You are right, Rob," she said. "I am sorry it has been this long. I should have spoken before. You should not wait any more."

"You mean . . . ?"

"I mean that you should find someone else. I am still not ready. Probably I never shall be."

She turned from me and started up the trail to her father's house. I caught up with her and we walked together but in silence. We broke into the upper meadow and looked down at the house and the road and the river beyond. The mountains rose behind us in a blend of evergreen, turning hardwoods and a cap of wind-cleaned rocks to which there clung a twisted pine or two. The Adirondacks were old and scarred and they had been abused, but there was newness coming. There was work

41

to be done and I was doing it, just as my father had done, but my father had had my mother and I had no one.

Helen started down the slope but I took her arm.

"It is not enough," I said. "I deserve more than this. Every plan I've made since I was 16 has been based on you. Everything I've built into the house my father left me has been built for you. If you tell me you don't love me anymore and will never love me again, I will accept this and I will go. Is that what you are saying, Helen?"

"No," she replied, "but maybe that is best for you to think. Leave me alone, Rob. It's not a cut-and-dried thing that has come between us, a time or an hour when you did this or that and so made me see I didn't care for you. If it had been, I would have told you."

"What is it then?"

"A need. A need for the strength which I don't have but which I could find if it were needed."

"But Helen, I have a need. I've told you that."

"Need is not something to tell of."

I picked up a dead branch from a tree and hurled it at a boulder which had been bedded since time began.

"I am not a poet," I said, "that can look for meanings where there are none. I am a mountain boy who runs a sawmill and you have given me, in this, no answer at all."

"I am sorry," she said.

She started off then. She walked down the slope alone.

I let her get into the house before I headed for the road. I was raging at her inside, or maybe I was raging at myself.

I thought: Where does she get the right to put her mind in the clouds and speak in riddles? She's a plain woman. Her father works the timber like everyone else. There have been no ministers, no professors in her family. What is she looking for? A prince, maybe, in golden clothes out of a fairy story?

I needed company. I needed a drink. I needed to go into the woods and cut and sweat and burn out my anger against the wolf beeches and the oaks, but it was Sunday night and there was no place to go but home.

It was the next morning that Jim Purdie, Helen's father, was killed. It's a hard time for a woodsman to die, when the first touches of cool fall weather make the balsam odor stronger and the axe cut cleaner. A woodsman should die in the winter when the forest is harsh and cold and offers nothing but cruel wind and long misery.

Jim Purdie died in the fall. He went into the woods and he felled a big pine tree and he started to limb it out. He was joking with his helper and he turned his head. A pinned hardwood sapling, stubborn in its strength, worked loose from under its crushed neighbor and snapped upright like a released catapult. It caught Jim Purdie under the ear and he died right there.

When I got the word, I knew that if Helen was ever going to need me, this was the time.

I shut down the sawmill and took off across the fields without even going back to my empty house to change my clothes. I beat the sawdust from my shoulders as best I could, then took off my hat and slammed it against the gate post as I turned in the drive. I figured Jim Purdie would understand my haste and know I would pay my full respects after I had given what comfort I could to those whom he had left behind. He had been an understanding man.

If I hadn't been quite so savage mad at the way Helen Purdie seemed to deny me a straight, clean answer the day before, I might have remembered how her father had done the same thing to me six months ago. I remembered it now as I sorrowed for him.

He was passing the mill and he stopped in to see me. He stood beside me as I pushed the cut.

The saw was running true and easy and clean.

All at once there was a crash and a scream and I dropped to the mill deck as Andy Caruthers yelled.

We shut down and we looked. There was a buried grapple point in the log. Andy pointed to the wall where the saw bits had ripped jagged holes after flying past where I had been.

"I'm shaking all over," he said. "I thought that was it."

"What do you mean 'thought?' " I said. "That was it. That saw is all finished. I don't know where I'm going to get a new one."

Jim Purdie looked at me. "Andy meant you," he said.

"I can take care of myself," I said.

"Yes," he replied. "I see you can. How are you getting along with Helen these days?"

I looked at Andy. He walked away. "Not too well," I told Jim.

"Her mother and I used to have a saying about what I'm trying to tell you," he said. "Love is in the winter. Would you know what that meant?"

"No."

Jim Purdie, that day, had been a burly, sweaty man with a stubble on his face and a tear in his pants. I figured I could solve any puzzle he put to me, but I had thought about that one and I couldn't solve it. I was always going to ask him more, but he was dead now and it was too late.

I went in the back door because I always had, at the Purdie home. Jim's boy, Joe, was sitting on the back steps alone where he didn't have to talk to anyone. He was 12, he had lost his mother before he had really known her and he had lost his father that day. There wasn't much I could do for him except put my hand on his shoulder as I went past. He was thinking things out and there was no place for me as yet. There might be.

Helen was standing by the kitchen stove. She was alone in the world with a 12-year-old brother to take care of, but she wasn't looking for any help either. I reached out to draw her close and hold her for a minute, but she moved away and put out her hands to fend me off.

"Helen," I said, and then I stopped. I didn't know any more.

I loved Helen Purdie, but she knew it. This was no time to repeat it. I had loved her father, too, and I was sorry from my heart that he was gone, but I couldn't find a way to tell her that. I looked for some softness in her eyes that would let me see a strong man might break through with the comfort that was needed, but her eyes were calm.

I just stood there, then, conscious of my old clothes and the sawdust in my pants cuffs and my hands still stained with the pitch from the mill.

"Helen," I said, "my father was killed, too. I know how you feel."

"No, you don't," she said. "That's what's the matter. If you had the fear within you that I have, always, and you needed someone to share it with you, then I would be in your arms. You could help me now and I could give the promise of later help."

The whole bitter time that we had sparred with each other and torn at each other came rushing back to me. I remembered Jim Purdie's words about the winter and I had the whole reason for everything that had been my torment. It was a time for hushed words, with death in the house, but I lashed out, because it seemed to me my love came first.

"For God's sake, Helen," I said, "is it fear you're looking for rather than need? Why should you seek fear rather than strength to lean on?"

"You don't have it, do you Rob? You don't fear the widow-makers in the tall trees and the axe glancing from the hemlock knot?"

"No, I don't," I told her. "Nor can I see why it would be a good thing? Why should you want it?"

"Because fearful men look over their shoulders and watch for death. Because brave men plunge boldly in. Because, if I came to you and shared your world, I would know that I was the only one who watched for danger while you roared ahead and ranged out, fearing nothing."

"Was your father fearful?"

"Yes, he was. So was yours."

"Helen," I said, "I don't quite believe all this, but suppose I promised to be what you want?"

"Your promise would be idle words. I have been watching for a sign. I have not found it. It did not show after Tom Jordan was crippled while he stood next to you on the rollway. It did not show when your own saw went to pieces on the grapple point."

"Your father told you about that?"

"Yes," she said, "and I looked at you that night and you had no awareness. Some women would maybe have been proud of that, Rob, but I was only fearful. If your house is empty, find a braver woman than I to fill it. Find one that won't need to touch you in the twilight to make sure you're there."

I had had enough. "Maybe I will," I said.

She called to me as I left and I turned, thinking it might be something I wanted to hear.

"After a year or two, don't look too deep in her eyes," she said. "She might be braver than you like."

I felt awfully lonesome as I walked away from there.

At the funeral Helen announced she would be going to the city to get a job, but that she would be back the next summer to sell the house and move the furniture. I was there, of course, to say good-by to Jim Purdie, but I didn't try to talk to Helen. She knew there was no need for her to go anywhere with my house waiting for her to say the word. She knew this so I said nothing.

If there had just been something simple like another man, I would have fought him until the blood ran out of one of us, but it wasn't another man and it wasn't simple.

The autumn air began to bite a little more sharply. The snow showed on the mountaintops in the mornings. Helen Purdie took Joe and a few pieces of furniture and was gone between breakfast and dinner one day. I had a letter from Joe. He said they had a nice apartment and that he was going to a good school.

He said no word that would have helped the lingering loneliness in the night.

I read. I worked. I sat overlong some evenings with my Uncle Jake, drinking the tasteless things he brewed in the swamps. They had no appeal to me and they left an unpleasant morning regret.

I stayed late at the store where the men were gathered and I spoke when I was spoken to and I searched for the sense of what Helen had said.

"Andy," I asked my log-turner, "what is it that I should fear?"

"Poverty," he said. "Did you get the cedar contract? Are you going to close the mill?"

We were out of logs. "Yes, I am," I said. "Tomorrow will be the last day. We'll put away the gear. I'm sorry."

"You couldn't help it," he said. "I can go into the woods for Denniston. I can come back with you in the spring."

"Yes," I said. "Are you afraid in the woods, Andy?"

"Of course," he said.

He laughed. The two men beside him laughed, but they drew back and looked across the room.

"I'm not," I said, "and I hear that I should be."

"All true," Andy said.

He left shortly. So did the two who had turned away. So did I, but I don't think I slept as well as they.

I tried to think, in the mornings, of the things that could happen. I thought of the ledges to slip from or the chain-saw blades that could break or the axe that could deflect from its mark, but there was no reality in the thoughts because I knew these things would never happen, not on the crisp days that breathed life to the resting world.

I put thought from me and tried to think no more.

I had the cedar contract. I had 1,000 poles to cut and, by mid-January, I had them stump-piled five miles back in the woods. It was a cold winter. The frost formed on the axe handle during a half hour break at noon. The shaft on the oil pump on my tractor sheared off when I started the motor one morning, and I burned out the bearings before I knew anything was wrong.

I had no time to fix tractors. There was a time limit on the cedar. I thought of Jim Purdie's old tractor sitting up there in the barn in back of his empty house. I wrote to Helen Purdie. I told her I was borrowing her tractor. I told her it was a lonesome winter. I told her I still loved her.

I met Andy Caruthers in the store the next evening. "You working alone?" he asked.

"Yes," I told him.

"Dangerous thing in the winter," he said. "You cut an artery or you get a limb on your head or a tree jumps the stump. When you're all alone, you're going to be right there."

"You do any of these with a friend right beside you, you're right there anyway, mostly."

"Yes," he said, "there's that, I suppose."

I went home to a cold house. It was 10 below zero the next morning. I had two loads of posts out to the road at 11 o'clock.

I took a slug of coffee from the thermos I kept in my truck and I headed back into the woods with the tractor.

The big wheels squeaked on the snow and the foot rest was glazed over with moisture from my boot. The air was sharp and the staccato bursts from the popping cylinders echoed back in a tone that means winter. I could feel the frost seeping in under my parka as I rode.

I snapped the tractor around in a wide circle when I came to my loading area. I brought the scoot up to the piled posts. I was half standing to escape the chill from the cold seat, my right foot slipped and I fell forward into the snow. The tractor kept moving.

I rolled over once, thinking I was clear, but then that big rear wheel clamped down hard on my left leg, halfway between my ankle and my knee, and I felt a hard, grinding pain. Then the front wheel of the tractor hit a hummock and the engine went dead.

I squirmed around to look at my leg. It was pinned under the wheel and the wheel was supporting a few hundred pounds and I knew I was in trouble.

My leg was shooting sparks up to my hip. I tried to pull just a little, hoping the cleats were in the right position so I could squeeze out from under. I couldn't. I was nailed to the ground.

I raised up to a sitting position and grabbed hold of a wheel spoke and threw all the weight I could muster against it. I couldn't turn it, not from where I was. I groped around for a stick or a pole that I could reach out with and pry, but there wasn't anything close, nothing I could move.

The woods were awfully quiet. The only sound except for my breathing was the snapping of the tractor engine as the steel contracted from the cold and a woodpecker pounding away at a tree nearby.

I looked at the tractor, then, and for the first time in my life I felt a cold seeping through me that wasn't that of the frost and the snow. It was the coldness of fear, and I knew that, from then on, it would be a part of my life because, if I ever got out of this fix, I would have the memory of it always.

The pain in my leg was getting less and less all the time. I thought I knew why. The part below the pressure point was probably half frozen already.

It would be 15 or 20 below zero when the weak sun went down. I knew I couldn't possibly live until morning. I was five miles back in the woods. Nobody expected me home, nobody would worry about me. By the time somebody did, it wouldn't matter.

My nose was losing feeling and so were my ears. I stomped my free foot against the tractor wheel, got my thumbs out of their pockets in my mittens and worked them around with the rest of my hand. I set my teeth, finally, and pulled hard at my pinioned leg. The pain started up with a rush and I stopped pulling and lay back in the snow, but when I did I felt panic and fright and, I think, the light touch of death.

I pulled myself up to a sitting position again and I hunched my shoulders over and beat my hands around my body and down my legs as far as I could reach. I thumped my finger tips against my chest. I cupped my hands over my face and exhaled in sharp bursts. The feeling came back into my nose with a painful burning. I grabbed that tractor spoke and I thrust out at it until I could feel the iron cut through my mitten, but nothing moved.

I was tired, then, and I lay back on the ground. I fumbled for a cigarette and, somehow, I got it lighted. I shut my eyes for a minute, but there were bright flashes across them under my eyelids and my brain was trying to do about six things at once, including thinking me out of there and solving something about Helen Purdie that I had been vaguely focussing on for about 10 minutes. There was something I had to tell her but she wasn't there and I was too sleepy to go and look for her. I figured I'd tell her later when I went over to her house to see her that night.

My cigarette was burning my mitten and my back was cold so I sat up again and shook my head and remembered where I was and that I wasn't going to Helen's that night and that was too bad, because I had a nice message for her. I wanted to tell her she was right and she was wrong, because I hadn't been afraid but I had needed her just the same. I wanted to tell her that love is in the winter when the air is sharp and the ground is cold and a man has the doing of what he has to do because no man who is a man can let the fears of a woman swerve him from his dreams.

I lay back again and I thought: Dear God, so now I have found the fear of which she spoke and I know what she meant because I surely need her now. I thought: What a strange place to find fear or the looks of fear, in the soft woods with a fearless woodpecker storming at the bark on the mighty trees and the rabbits running around and looking at me strangely and waiting to take me home.

It was getting dark, but I didn't care because I was nice and warm. My hand was beating across my chest and I thought: What a silly thing for a hand to do. That hand will scare the woodpecker away, if there is a woodpecker.

The hand stopped and the woodpecker flew far out in a black field and I went to sleep. I dreamed Helen Purdie had been there but she was walking away and leaving me because I was a stubborn fool who deserved what he was getting. Her brother Joe wasn't walking away, though. He was shaking me.

"That's good," I said, "you stay for awhile."

But, as he leaned over me, there was a roaring from the tractor and the blue smoke coiled up behind and I felt another pain in my leg down somewhere beneath me, and some one was still shaking me and rolling me. I looked up and I felt the realness of a woollen coat, and I made an effort and I separated the black from the white, and I sat up. I started to flail my arms, but I was tired after a little while and I was warm enough.

Then I was lying on some poles on the scoot and the scoot was crunching the snow down in front of its runners, and I was pounding my hands on the poles and they were starting to hurt a little. My head was on somebody's lap, but it wasn't Joe Purdie's because Joe was driving the tractor wide open, sitting up straight on the seat and ducking his head for the snow-bowed branches. Somebody leaned over me and gave me a long kiss and I wanted to say, "Don't do that because I'm waiting for Helen.

But I didn't say anything because I needed to be kissed and anyway it was Helen.

I was in my own kitchen, lying on the floor and smelling whiskey and coffee and the reason I was smelling it was because it was in my mouth and I was drinking it. I had a pillow under my head and I hurt all over and someone was hurting me more all the time by pounding me and rubbing me. My fingers were warm from the coffee cup but they were too far away from me to be getting the cup to my mouth, but still I was drinking coffee.

I raised up on my elbow and looked at Helen Purdie. She'd been gone for 100 years, but she was still pretty. I told her so.

"Lie still," she said. "I've called the doctor."

"Just tell me this," I said, "what are you doing away from a nice warm apartment saving a man's life in the bitter woods?"

"I found out I still feared for you even when I was nowhere near," she said. "I found out I didn't care whether you needed me or not, because I needed you. I got your letter yesterday and I came up this morning."

"Why did you come in on the trail?"

"Something told me to," she said. "Your fire was out and, weather like this, a man should come home to his lunch if he's where he's able to. I was worried."

"That's good," I said. "Stay worried. It's a comforting thing to have a worrier at home. That's the doctor's car. Let him in."

Joe filled the stove again while the doctor worked. It was roaring red. The heat filled the kitchen in little waves and ripples.

"Doc," I asked, "could I get married tomorrow?"

He chuckled. "No. You're going to be laid up for a couple of weeks. That foot is pretty bad. You better wait until spring anyway. Spring is the time for weddings."

"Three days," said Helen, "it takes three days. I don't want to wait until spring."

I smiled at her. "Neither do I," I said. "Love is in the winter."

"If you're going to be laid up for awhile," said Joe, "would you want me to put those posts out to the road for you? I could do it after school and on Saturdays."

"No," I said, "it's too dangerous working alone in the woods. You better wait until I can help you."

"What could happen?" he asked.

"I don't know," I told him, "but I don't want to be worrying about you."

I looked over at Helen and she smiled in her turn.   ■

Go Ahead and Smoke

"Come right in," said the man. "Come right in. Sit here. It's good to see you. Wait a minute. I'll get you an ash tray."

"I don't need one," I said. "I'm only going to stay a minute. I don't need to smoke."

"It's all right. Be comfortable. Myra, don't we have something for Bill's cigarette ashes?"

"I don't need anything. I don't want to smoke."

He laughed. "I know better," he said. "We want you to feel at home. I know you smokers. I used to smoke myself. . . . smoked all the time. Why, I smoked. . . . "

"Five packs a day and three cigars and you chewed in between times," I said. "Then, one day, you cut it out. . . . JUST LIKE THAT."

"How'd you know?"

"You just made up your mind to quit and you quit. . . . BANG."

"My goodness, how in the world could you guess that?"

"I'm psychic," I said. I didn't add that I'm also kind hearted. It hurts these multitudes of masterful men if you tell one of them that every non-smoker in the world claims to have been steeped in the stuff for years, saturated with it, ear oozing with it, and then quit smoking between puffs, stopped as suddenly as a kiddy-car hitting a cliff.

His wife handed me a saucer, a china saucer with hand painted roses on it. "You go ahead and smoke," she said.

"Honestly, I don't need to smoke."

"Ha, Ha," she said. "You're probably just gasping for a smoke right now. Go ahead. Go ahead and smoke."

I had a little cold and my stomach was empty and my mouth was still hot from the cigarette I'd thrown out when I knocked at their door. I didn't want a cigarette any more than a sailor with a girl in town wants the gangway watch. But they were eyeing me as eagerly as a tourist from Hooper's Falls watches a hired addict in a Chinatown Opium Den. So I did my duty.

"That's better," said the woman. "Gracious me, Sidney and I don't mind smokers. Sidney used to smoke. He smoked five packs of cigarettes a day and.... "

"We've already played that scene," I said. "It's time now for you to tell me that you can get rid of the cigarette smell without any trouble."

"How did you ever know that?"

"He's psychic," said the man.

"Amazing," she said. "We can, you know. We get rid of the smell with no trouble at all. We open the windows and doors and Sidney has this big fan that he carries from room to room while I spray Scootsmell on the drapes and the furniture. Then we wipe the baseboards and the radiators with Superspruce in hot water. And the throw rugs are easy. We found out about the throw rugs from a letter in Roberta's Remedies."

"I'm interested," I said. "What about the throw rugs?"

"You dip them in mange cure and lemon juice," she said.

"So it's no trouble at all?"

"No trouble. Besides, we don't mind cigarette smoke, really. Why, Sidney used to smoke in the house. Sidney smoked.... "

"Five packs. Yes. Now, what I came to see you about was.... Oh, I'm sorry ... I'm terribly sorry.... "

"What's the matter? Oh ... Well, don't you worry about that old saucer. Don't you worry at all. How could you know that the paint would melt off the roses when you ground out that cigarette? It doesn't matter. That saucer is just an old thing that my mother's sister painted while she was in the hospital that time with Rusterholstitus. She was very active, right to the end, and she knew I adored roses, so she painted that saucer for me."

"And now I've spoiled it," I said. "Really, I don't. . . . "

"Please," she said. "It wasn't professional art, you know. The poor old dear was terribly sick. The nurses said it was only pure determination that kept her working on those roses. She wasted right away, you know. But she hoarded all her strength for her painting sessions. She finished the saucer two days before she died. So don't worry about it."

"Well," I said, "I stopped in to see if. . . . "

"Have another cigarette," she said. "You don't look comfortable. Go ahead and smoke. We don't mind. We know you want to smoke. But maybe I'll just get you something else for an ashtray. Wait . . . you're not leaving, are you?"

But I already had. I was running low on cigarettes.   ■

Ask Daddy for Diamonds

My neighbor stood on my porch with his obnoxious off-spring, Alice and Andrew, aged seven and eight.

"It's an emergency," he said, "and we can't get a sitter."

"Hit the kids over the head," I said, "and chain them to the kitchen stove."

"Don't you want to help out in an emergency?"

"I'd rather be dipped gradually into hot grease," I said. "But I'll sacrifice myself for a half-hour ... No more ... "

The half-hour had stretched to two and a half. I had already decided that such lack of consideration must be avenged. Then Andrew popped Alice on the button and Alice threw a book at Andrew, unfortunately missing him by a foot.

I decided that it was story time.

"I'm going to tell you about the wise men," I said. "I'm going to tell you about the wise men who followed the star."

"Stars don't move," said Andrew. "How could they follow a star when a star can't move?"

"In those days, stars moved," I said.

"The earth moves," he said. "We learned that in school. The earth turns over and over. It turns like this."

He lay down on the rug and showed me how the earth turns. Alice lay down and turned, too. She turned against Andrew and Andrew swung a fair left and caught her in the ribs and she grabbed his arm and bit him. She drew blood and I smiled.

Andrew didn't yell. He looked at the tooth marks. "I'll probably get blood poisoning," he said quietly. "I'll probably die and go to heaven."

I wasn't that optimistic about his chances or mine.

"Your mother will fix it when you get home," I said. "You sit down now and I'll tell you about the wise men."

"Stars don't move," he said. "The teacher told us that stars don't move."

"Can you spell disestablishmentarianism?" I asked.

"No."

"I thought so," I said. "Schools spend their time teaching nonsense about stars and don't teach spelling. Don't you know that if the earth turned, we'd all fall off and spin through space?"

"Like an astronaut?"

"Sure. Except we wouldn't have any nice ships and food pills and oxygen. We'd fall and fall and then we'd starve to death."

"Probably our teacher doesn't know that," he said.

"So now," I said, having solved one teacher's problem about what to do the next day, "I'll tell you about the wise men who followed the star. You know about Christmas, don't you?"

"Sure. Santa Claus comes."

I considered that. It didn't seem right to let him persist in this fallacy. A person should tell kiddies the truth.

"Santa Claus," I said, "is your father."

"Honest? You mean he can bring me presents?"

"Really and truly?" asked Alice.

I looked at my watch. Three hours had passed. Justice is justice. I did my duty.

"Sure," I said. "Your old man . . . your father is Santa Claus and he can get you anything you want. All you have to do is to keep on asking for it. Ask him every day because he's got a lot of things to remember and he might forget."

I heard the car in the drive. "What are you going to ask for?" I demanded.

"A diamond ring," said Alice.

"Good. You might just as well have earrings, too. You should have earrings and a necklace and a few new dresses. . . . ."

" . . . and a bicycle," said Andrew.

" . . . with a motor and headlights and a portable television set on the handlebars," I said. "Well, good-night."

I pushed them at their father as he entered. "Sorry we're a little later than we thought," he said.

"It's all right," I said.

"We won't forget this," he told me.

He won't, either. I'm sure he won't. He'll remember it for a long, long, long time. ■

Uncle Oscar's Magic Touch

My Uncle Oscar loved the things that grew from the soil. He picked the pin cherries carefully in clusters and his touch was tender as he took the berries from the bush. When he gathered violets, he was as careful of the stems as of the blooms.

He put all these beautiful things in crocks and covered them lovingly with sugar and yeast and water. He was possibly more appreciative of what nature provided than was any other man in Cedar River. He knew there was a potential key to paradise in everything that bloomed.

Nature rewarded Oscar for his devotion. She worked in a mellow manner on the substance in his crocks, performing feats of alchemy that converted even the humble dandelions and tender black birch twigs into fluids that brightened the sun and brought the stars closer to the evening river.

On a bushel of arbutus blooms that Uncle Oscar set to brewing one spring, nature did such a superb job that when Oscar was induced by promoters of civic betterment to part with a gallon of the blessed beverage for a town treat, the entire population walked in the mist with the muses and everyone spoke in iambic pentameter for a week.

Occasionally Oscar was driven by economic need to produce beverages for the market, but at those times he made no pretense of artistry. He worked with a fierce savagery akin to that of an artist who hires out to paint a barn.

He didn't use the harvest of groves or gardens in his commercial ventures. He threw garbage and grain and molasses and

59

yeast into tubs to ferment and then distilled the horrible result. He put this into syrup tins and rushed downriver to sell
it before it dissolved the containers. He resented the whole
deal.

Fortunately, Oscar's financial pressures were few. He could
end most of them by gentle swindles or by borrowings from the
innocent. He also got a little cash from the sale of his blissful,
lovingly concocted brews to a selected customer list.

It was for the sake of these customers, he claimed, as well as
to keep his own soul pure, that he was constantly pleading for
the preservation of humus and the plowing in of organic sub-
stances. He wanted the earth to retain its richness.

He said, "All you farmers are trustees of the soil. You ought to
be ashamed of abusing it."

He scolded Deak Trembley in public for growing small fruits
that were less than perfect. "You ain't mulched your raspberries
in three years," he told Deak. "You ain't trimmed your grapes,
neither."

"Why should I?" asked Deak. "Somebody always steals them
just when they're hitting the peak of ripeness."

"That's a selfish way to talk," said Oscar. "Some poor guy
works hard in the night to gather them and he's got a right to
expect them to be juicy, not small and shameful."

Deak questioned this philosophy. He denied his responsi-
bility to crooks. So Oscar had to put up with Deak's selfishness,
or at least he chose to for the sake of keeping Deak from getting
too solidly founded suspicions about what was happening to
his grapes. It was probably for the same reason that Oscar kept
Deak on his list of beverage customers.

Deak appreciated being one of Oscar's selections for surplus
buying. He even defied his wife when she tried to end his
favored relationship with the master distiller and blender.

Except for a bit of dutiful nagging, Annie Trembley was tolerant of Deak's activities. She had never been a masterful
woman. But after Deak got himself saved at a revival meeting
one year, she developed the absurd idea that he should stay
saved.

She figured he might have a chance if he stayed away from the Devil's recruiting agents, particularly Uncle Oscar. Deak protested this notion.

"It ain't that I'm a bosom pal of Oscar's," said Deak. "It's just that I like to do a little trading with him, here and there, for this and that."

"Oscar only trades in one thing," said Annie. "His trading is immoral and illegal and he cheats you anyway."

Deak didn't mind being accused of breaking moral or statutory laws. He hated to be hailed as a poor trader, though.

"I get my money's worth," he said. "What's a few dollars compared with a fresh outlook on problems?"

"You can get a fresh outlook any Sunday in church," said Annie.

That appeal failing, Annie's next step was to try to stop the traffic from the other end. She caught Oscar in the store and explained that she didn't want to have Deak refueled for flying.

"Deak doesn't need any help from your vile bottles," she said. "Deak can get all the help he needs from a better source."

Uncle Oscar was puzzled. In the first place, he rarely had bottles. For his prime stock he used jugs and fruit jars. In the second place, he hadn't heard about any competition.

"What better source?" he asked Annie. "Who else around here is making liquor?"

"I mean," said Annie, "that when Deak feels downcast or tested beyond his strength, he can get help from heaven."

"Heaven is helping Deak?"

"Both of us. We've both put ourselves in heaven's hands. If we're in trouble or need anything, heaven will send help."

Oscar didn't argue. He wasn't in a position to check Annie's statement with her announced benefactor. So Annie took her store purchases and started for the door. A wandering dog got tangled in her feet. Down she went.

She clung tightly to both bags as she fell. But she found herself unable to rise with both arms thus engaged. "Don't just stand there," she said to Oscar. "I need some help."

"From me?" asked Uncle Oscar. "Gosh, you just said you'd be getting it from heaven."

The loungers roared but Annie wasn't bested.

"I would be," she said, "except that the good Lord certainly isn't going to work any miracles while the Devil has a spy around to watch how he does it."

Thus outworded by a woman, Uncle Oscar's dignity demanded that he avoid future encounters with her. He dropped Deak from his sales list, shaking his head firmly when approached with a plea.

"I ain't selling to nobody that don't manure his crops," said Oscar. "You fit so good with heaven, let it rain you some communion wine." ■

The Uses of Danger

He was just a little boy. The sweat was pouring down from his forehead and his face looked red and overexposed. He was digging a hole in the vacant lot, probing with a bar and struggling with a shovel. It was a long-handled, round-pointed shovel and it was seven or eight inches taller than he was.

I walked over. "Digging for water?" I asked.

He gave me a look that all small boys reserve for nosy grownups.

"A dugout hut, maybe?" I asked.

"No," he said, "I'm just digging a hole . . . just for fun . . . just digging a hole."

That's how I knew it was a dugout hut. When an inquisitive adult happens to hit on the truth, a small boy HAS to lie. Thus the sin is really on the soul of the adult, because if the adult continued to guess wrongly, the boy could stay silent.

"I used to cover mine with boards and tar paper," I said. "If I was going to build one now, I'd use a piece of tin, like that one over there. . . . "

"That's what . . . " he said. He stopped. He scowled.

"I'm sorry," I said. I took four or five steps away and then he called to me.

"How'd you keep the sides from caving in?" he said.

"If you set boards against the dirt and drive stakes to hold them, it'll work pretty well. You going to have a floor?"

"I got an old rug," he said.

"Old rug's the best thing there is," I told him.

"Aren't you going to tell me that a dugout hut's dangerous?"

"I will if you want me to. I thought you knew it was dangerous. Sure it's dangerous. It wouldn't be any fun if it wasn't dangerous."

"Probably it'll cave in and bury me," he said.

"Probably. But you can stick your head out and then you can breathe. You can holler and somebody will dig you out."

"That's right. Suppose somebody is walking around here at night and falls in?"

"I don't think they'd do any more than break a leg or an arm," I told him. "Besides, people who walk around vacant lots at night are just looking for trouble."

"Did your mother let you build dugout huts?" he asked.

"No. She told me they were dangerous and that people might fall into them at night."

We stood looking at each other. "But I built them anyway," I said.

Then I turned again and walked off. Behind me I could hear him laugh and then laugh louder. That was good. I knew I had made a friend. Of course, when he quoted me to his mother, I would then make an enemy, but a person can't expect to do much better than to have friends and enemies balance up.

And in the summer it is needful for a boy to have a little advice once in awhile from non-parental adults. Summer is activity time and the trouble with most modern small boy activity is that it is supervised and safety-ized until it is no more fun than reading "Lady Chatterly's Lover" at a permissive pre-primary school.

If a small boy is limited to legality in his summer fun, he is liable to lapse into complete lethargy. Organized leisure time activity never produced a Thomas Edison. It is more likely to produce the mediocrity that falls victim to Madison Avenue and the Jack Paar Show.

Before the Little League coaches and the Cub Pack parents jump in hard with their spikes flashing, I suppose I should qualify that. There isn't anything immoral about a few controls and perhaps a rule or two. But a boy on the dead run from planned activity to planned activity, is a boy who doesn't have time to exercise his brain. ■

Foreclosure Man

James King, expert business analyst, had come face to face with his old home town. He was sitting in the corporation-affairs offices of the Jefferson National Bank in New York City. The town had come to him. He was working on the portfolio of Maspreth Motors, chief industry of Schonowie on the Tannerkill. When he was a boy Maspreth Motors had represented everything in the world that was solid and wealthy and dignified and secure. The economy of Schonowie had centered around it. Maspreth had manufactured plows and pumps and generators. For one glorious interval they had manufactured cars; but that had been a brief thing, a mere fling, and they had had to yield that business to the overpowering pressures of the big three.

He hoped that there wasn't anything very wrong with Maspreth. If there were, Schonowie was all finished as a town. He didn't know why that should bother him, but it did.

As he read the figures before him he realized that it didn't matter what he hoped. Maspreth Motors was in trouble. It hadn't made any real money since 1917. It had been running on company capital until there was no more. Then it had been running on bank loans. Even in the lush days of the Second World War Maspreth had barely crept into the black.

He checked for high owners' salaries. There were none. There were no big dividends, no treasury raiding, no personal plundering. Maspreth was just dead on its feet. It was the old story of an inefficient, paternal company in a friendly but unbusinesslike town. There was no place for such companies in the efficiency of the atomic age.

65

He picked up his pencil to make a start on the exposure of facts that would bring the bank ax down on the neck of Maspreth. He was interrupted. Charles Simmons was at his shoulder.

"Let's go to lunch," said Simmons. He took a look at the folder in front of James King. "Maspreth Motors, eh?" he said.

Charles Simmons was King's immediate supervisor. They went to lunch often. Simmons was a veteran of years of jockeying for the plush positions in the bank organization. He never lunched alone. He knew that many secrets are exposed in relaxation. He filed such things away. At dessert he spoke again of Maspreth Motors.

"That thing shouldn't ever have got to your desk," he said. "The old man put it in the works himself. It's a routine foreclosure, but he's got a soft spot for that bunch. He hopes you'll spot something. You won't."

James King admired Mr. Hornsby—"the old man." He knew Simmons was after Hornsby's job. He had no love for Simmons, and he had no intention of giving him any weapons. "Is Hornsby a friend of the Maspreths?" he asked.

"You haven't read very far, have you? There aren't any Maspreths—not in the company. They sold out to a group of young engineers about six years ago. That's when we went in. Somebody talked Hornsby into helping the boys along. The directors have been pretty hot about it for the last couple of years. How does it look to you?"

"Just fair," said James cautiously.

Simmons snorted. "Fair, hell! That isn't what I heard. Hornsby pulled a boner and he hates to admit it. You'll find out when you get in deeper. Well, match you for the check?"

James King won. It was his sole bright spot in a dismal day.

He worked two hours that afternoon before he reduced the Maspreth figures to a presentable form. Maspreth Motors owed the bank one hundred and thirty thousand dollars. For security there were only the buildings, the water turbines, the name, the machinery and the rights to a new world-beating gadget that was not yet on the market. Four years ago Maspreth had come up with plans for a combination chain saw, lawn mower, trimmer and paint sprayer that promised large sales to suburban home owners, but it was not yet perfected. Probably it never would be.

He picked up a report form and wrote, "There is no real reason why we do not move in on this company. All it has is an indefinite potential."

Then he sat for another half hour and looked through the walls of his office and saw the little town in the hills. He saw the mill dam and the grass-banked river by the tall-stacked factory. He looked at the town and saw that it was good, and he hated to sign his name to its death warrant.

Then he saw something else. He saw himself at seventeen, in 1938, proudly guiding a Maspreth Special Six to a home on a quiet street, steering it with one hand because the other arm was busy holding a honey-blond high-school junior beside him—Susan Kendall! He hadn't thought of Susan Kendall since 1947, when he'd heard that she'd married someone in Chicago. Or had it been the memory of Susan Kendall that had kept him single and purposeful and alone?

He shook that off; but it was because he remembered Susan Kendall and because he remembered that old Maspreth Special Six and because he suddenly knew that those years with the two of them had been his last true happiness that he took his pencil again and wrote another line on his report.

"I recommend that we hold off for another six months and see if, in that time, their new machine makes their prospects look better."

That was the best he could do, the closest he could come to turning back the clock. As he clipped the papers together he wondered how he had come to leave all the old things behind. He knew that he would never find the answer because the answer was buried in a host of his past needs and wants and indefinable desires. He knew it was too late to change. The years had passed, and the water had flowed, and his need for Susan and Schonowie had given way long ago to his need for security and success.

He knew all this, but he was still not surprised that his sleep that night was troubled and broken.

The next morning he was savagely underlining the facts that showed the flaws in a company over in Jersey when the intercom buzzed and Hornsby himself summoned him.

"I have your report on Maspreth Motors, King," he said. "It is comprehensive and it is completely puzzling. Why the conflict?"

"Well, sir, I suppose I couldn't make up my mind to toss Maspreth to the wolves. You see, Schonowie is my home town. I hate to think of that factory going under. I used to think of Maspreth as being something special. Did you ever see one of their cars?"

"They haven't made cars for over thirty years."

"No, sir, but they used to. I had one of them. It was quite old when I got it; but the fenders were solid, and the paint was good. I paid seventy-five dollars for it. It had a sleeve-valve motor. It purred."

He checked himself. Mr. Hornsby was smiling. He realized that he had been sounding maudlin. "All I mean, Mr. Hornsby, is that I suppose that's why the report was puzzling. I'm biased. I know that isn't a banker's attitude——"

"Of course it's a banker's attitude."

"Sir?"

"Who told you that bankers were supposed to be bloodless?" He didn't wait for an answer. He smiled and went on. "It happens that I'm prejudiced about this one myself. I'm the man who got talked into the deal in the first place—not because I was sentimental, but because it looked good. I don't know what went wrong. I had Harris down there, but all he brought back were sour-looking facts. What about you? How would you like to go down there and take a good look?"

"I'm not a field man, Mr. Hornsby."

"No? Are you glued to that desk? You're not married, are you, King? Live alone? Someplace like the Essex Arms?"

"It is the Essex Arms."

"Then why in tunket aren't you a field man if I want you to be? Nobody's waiting dinner for you. You leave for Schonowie today."

"Yes, sir."

"I don't know how you get there. Probably on a horse. When you look at that company see if there's any logical reason to follow your suggestion about another six months. Take a week. I'm supposed to be reporting to the committee, but I can hold them off that long—lack of time, lack of typists, other business. See Meeker. He'll give you funds to draw on. Now get out of here; I have a coffee meeting."

Simmons was out somewhere. James King laid the Jersey portfolio on his desk and wrote, "Called out of town for a week," on the memo pad and went home to pack.

Schonowie was a hard town to get to. James had to hire a drive-yourself car in Albany. He was amused to find that the only thing available was a new convertible.

He spent the night in Albany and arrived at Schonowie in the early midmorning. All the way down the valley, over and around the ridges, the September sun and the holiday feeling of the car worked on his tenseness until he found himself almost in a holiday mood.

He found that the landmarks of Schonowie had not changed. The leisurely attitude of the town hadn't changed, either. The shoppers on the streets were indolent; the gas-station attendant didn't rush.

Then he found something else that was still the same. Susan Kendall was sitting in the office of Maspreth Motors.

If he hadn't known she was thirty-seven, he would have guessed her to be six or eight years younger. Her face still had a scrubbed look, and she didn't have the air of cool efficiency that distinguished receptionists at his bank. She had a big smile instead. At first he thought she didn't recognize him.

"There was a man just here from that bank," she said as he gave her his card.

He played it straight. "I know," he said. "I'm another man."

Then she held out her hand. "Jimmy King," she said. "It's been a long time."

"A long time," he agreed.

"Kenneth was saying just the other night——"

"Your brother Kenneth? Is he here? I thought he was with Allied Electric."

"He was. He's with Maspreth now. He's fifteen per cent owner. That means he owes fifteen per cent of the notes. He likes it better, though. He said . . . "

It was two hours before he thought about anything but hometown news. By twelve o'clock he was ready to start on the company books, but then it was time for lunch. They hung a sign on the door, a refreshing change from the bank, where there were relief clerks for the relief clerks, and they went up street to the diner. They seemed to hurry, but it was two-thirty before they got back.

He assuaged his conscience by telling himself that he was learning intimate details about the company. He was. He was learning other things too.

He learned that the company was presently manufacturing all the parts to the combination tool except the chain saw, which still had bugs. He learned that Susan had been working there for three years.

She had returned home to take care of her mother in a last illness and she had stayed home long enough to realize that Chicago's high pay for secretaries could not compete with Schonowie's milder social life and placid ways. The rumor of her marriage had been false, although she admitted that she had been three times on the verge.

"The last one was the nicest," she said, "but he would never have fitted in Schonowie. He was big town. I used to take three hours getting dressed when he took me to dinner."

James King wondered how long she had taken that morning. He couldn't see that there was any room for improvement. He told her so.

"I should protest about that," she said, "but I won't. I suspect it's true. I feel good all the time, so I suppose I look good. That's Schonowie, Jimmy. Don't you remember how all the middle-aged women looked rosy-cheeked and young?"

"No, I don't," he said, "but I remember something else. That dance dress of yours. Wasn't it aquamarine?"

"Dance dress? Aquamarine?" She looked closely at him then, and there was perhaps a little mist in her eyes. "Jimmy," she said, "Jimmy, you old——Not the dress, Jimmy—just the sash. The dress was pink. You sent me Talisman roses. How did you remember that?"

"I remember a lot of things," said James King, "even if I don't understand them."

She changed the focus. "Tell me about you," she said.

James avoided the subject of himself. "You tell me some more about Maspreth instead," he said. "I'm supposed to weigh the facts."

She told him about Maspreth. The company was controlled by five young engineers, three of them home-town boys, who had pooled their money and credit to buy out the last Maspreth six years ago. They were doing the best they could.

He sat there while she talked, but he wasn't listening. He looked at her blue eyes and at her retained youth, and he wondered what it was that he had had and had lost. He was thirty-seven years old and he had solid success just ahead of him, but he would have given up all this certainty right then for the haze of his unknown future when he was taking Susan home from the junior prom in his seventy-five-dollar Maspreth Special Six.

Another thought came to him then. He didn't have to live like a recluse at the Essex Arms. He could afford a home in the suburbs. He had passed the hurdles of economizing and nightly overtime. There was no real need for him to stay in the rut into which he had gradually fallen.

He looked at Susan's hair and at her tanned arms and at her big smile, and he missed about fifteen sentences about the condition and hopes of Maspreth Motors. He told himself that this didn't matter.

He tried to snap out of it that afternoon. He started to dig into Maspreth. He took a guided tour of the plant. He saw a rousing spirit in Maspreth's employees and saw that they all admired the trim smartness of Susan, but he couldn't see any signs of pending profit. There were a lot of things he didn't like. He couldn't find any supervisors, for instance. He learned that they were all on the test range, pooling their brains on the chain-saw attachment. It looked like a do-or-die operation, and solid companies don't thusly put all their eggs into one basket.

As he looked further he saw that Maspreth didn't have many baskets. Their generators were strictly small-output, farm-supply stuff. The gross sale of them wouldn't carry ten men. The company was still making replacement parts for pumps, but this didn't look like big business either.

The main effort was obviously on the production of the mower, trimmer and sprayer parts for the combination tool, and there was a great backlog of these parts—useless until the chain saw was perfected.

"That isn't good business, you know," he said to Susan. "They shouldn't be making all those parts. They should suspend production until the whole thing's ready to go."

"If they did that, these men wouldn't have anything to work on," she answered.

"Well, my gosh," he said, "they'd just have to——"

"They can't afford to lay off, Jimmy. That's the one thing Maspreth's always stood for—steady work. These men depend on Maspreth. The company's just got to keep them working."

"Even if the company goes bankrupt?"

"Maspreth's been in trouble before, Jimmy. When they were making cars and the market kept falling off and falling off, they thought they'd go bankrupt then too; but they got the generator business going, and it kept them alive. This new tool will save the company now."

James King wasn't so sure. He started back toward the office and then he saw the strangest thing of the afternoon. Making an island in the main lane of traffic through the plant was a big glass case, and in the case was a Maspreth Special Six. It was shiny and polished, and the glass of the case was washed.

"Monument to past glories?" he said to Susan.

"I don't know," she said. "I can't explain it. It means something to these men. They polish it during lunch hour every once in a while. It's been there since nineteen twenty-two."

"The same year as mine," he said. He found himself feeling a little glow as he peered through the glass at the gleaming old car.

"I don't know either," he said, "and I know darn well the bank wouldn't know. Let's get me back to work."

He was reluctantly digging into the assets and the open accounts when he and Susan were joined by two of the company engineers. One of them was Kenneth Kendall. He looked grim. The other was Arnold Houghton, who grabbed James King by the hand while they had a brief high-school reunion.

Then there was a silence, and he had to tell them the reason for his visit. He was apprehensive while he did it, for the atmosphere at Maspreth Motors had got so close to old home week that his pronouncement was a little like a young millionaire's sending his mother to the county farm.

"Look, Jim," said Kenneth. "If your boss is just trying to find a reason to carry us for another year or so, we've got plenty of reasons. We didn't do too badly this afternoon. In fact, we did well enough so that we're going to run another test tomorrow morning with a new clutch. We'll whip this thing. All we need is time. Tell them that."

He hesitated before answering. He looked at Susan Kendall and thought how nice she would look at a party of the bank office staff. Then he corrected himself, because he realized that she looked nicer right where she was. The trouble was that it didn't look as though she were going to get to stay there long— neither were these friendly, hard-working men. He spoke then, bluntly.

"I'm going to stay here for at least four or five days," he said, "and it looks to me as though that were all the time you had. If I tell them when I get back that you're all set to go on your new product, I think they'll go along. If not, Mr. Hornsby can't save you without risking his job; I can't save you no matter how much I risk, and I doubt if you can save yourselves."

They accepted that. If they thought that an old classmate should be able to get them more leeway time than four or five days, they didn't tell him so. They invited him to dinner.

James King was glum through the meal. He was a little brighter later in the evening when he took Susan out riding to see the old places in the quiet valley. The convertible helped. They drove with the top down and watched the stars on the rushing Tannerkill.

She was still living in the old family house. As James turned into the tree-lined street, it seemed to him as though he dropped years from his shoulders; but when he took her hand as he let her out, he knew the years were still there. A sport dress doesn't turn into a pink gown for the wishing, and neither of them was seventeen years old any more.

The next two days in Schonowie went by with the cool pace of fall days in a small town. He had gone through the Maspreth books so often that there was no further need to stay cooped up in the office. Susan let her work go too. She said if the saw succeeded she could get someone in to help her; and if it didn't, there wasn't any use in worrying anyway.

This philosophy was another thing that James King found difficult to reconcile with his last fourteen years among harder but less matter-of-fact people. He put it aside to be studied later. He didn't have time right then. He was busy enjoying the clean clear days in the colorful valley. He was busy reliving his youth.

With Susan he picnicked and drove the hills. They visited the fair at the county seat and they went to a local auction. James went to the cemetery to plant fresh flowers on his parents' graves. He dug deep into the loam and he set purple chrysanthemums that would last until the deepest of valley frosts. When he had finished, Susan took him by the hand and held it for a moment.

"Jim," she said, "I know I'm being bold. That's my Chicago training, I suppose. But why don't you stay here and help the men in that factory. They need someone like you. There isn't a one of them who's really a businessman. They don't know cost control or proper inventory procedure or tax structure. I can't help them much. I'm a good secretary, but I don't know the things they need help with. Aren't you ready to come home?"

He took her other hand so that he held them both. "Yes, I am, Susan," he said, "but it's too late. There isn't really any home to come to. You know that. These boys aren't going to be able to keep going. Businesses like this don't have a place any more. But look at it another way. Wouldn't you like to go and live near New York? I'm talking about getting married, Susan—you know that, don't you? Susan, we're not youngsters any more, but I think we could make it go."

She didn't answer for a minute. Then she shook her head. "No," she said. "I found out I wasn't Chicago and I wouldn't be New York either. This is my town."

"Your town isn't going to be here much longer, Susan."

"Then I'll stay as long as it is. You better take me back to the factory, Jimmy. If you really think it's falling apart, then I'd better be there to pick up the pieces."

This was the afternoon of the third day. They found Kenneth Kendall in the office, and with him were Arnold Houghton and a younger man who looked as though he were fresh out of engineering school. All three looked haggard, but they were still hopeful. The new clutch hadn't worked. They sat at different desks and discussed compositions and plastics, and they doodled on office stationery.

"I figure we've got time for one more good whack at it," said Kenneth. He turned to speak to James directly. "What we're up against, Jim, is the varying speeds of the various tools. We get a wear——"

That was when the telephone rang, and the telegram came in from Mr. Hornsby. It was for James King. "Report back at once. Will explain. No longer any need to check Maspreth Motors. Board decided yesterday to foreclose."

James put through a call to Mr. Hornsby, got a connection and got the full story. Mr. Hornsby hadn't been able to postpone a decision. Simmons' copy of the damning report of Maspreth's problems, summarized by James King on his last day at the office, had been included in a group of papers sent to the corporations committee. It had convinced them of Maspreth's failure.

"Simmons came in and apologized to me," said Mr. Hornsby dryly. "He said the report got in with some other papers by mistake. Someday I'll take an hour off and get enough on Simmons to hang him. Anyway, you'd better come home."

The Maspreth office was full of engineers by the time James King hung up. He explained. His stomach churned. He knew he would never make a field man. He knew his place was at a desk, working with cold figures—not in the midst of a bunch of disappointed people. He found himself hating Simmons, not only for letting these people suffer for his personal ambitions, but also for fixing it so that he, James King, would be in their midst when the disappointment came. He had been reconciled to their failure, but he had never thought that he would be the breaker of the bad news.

It was worse when they were nice people, when they didn't storm at him or seem to blame him personally for their plight. To hold them in this mood, he threw them the whole story of Simmons' treachery to Hornsby and thus also to them.

They didn't look surprised. "That's the sort of thing I came back here to get away from," said Arnold Houghton. "I sure hate to go back in it again."

"I suppose it's impossible for you to meet your current note?" James said.

Kenneth Kendall laughed. "Twenty thousand dollars?" he said. "We haven't got a thousand between us."

"I've got twenty thousand dollars," said James King. He said it automatically and he didn't know why he said it. For a moment he almost panicked and ran.

Then he saw Susan smile and he knew why he said it. It was because he was willing to back her wishes to the last dollar he owned. And then he smiled too, because he knew that this offer had been the key to his whole thinking about Susan. He loved her. He loved her to the point where he was not only willing to forgo success but even to buy his way into becoming a part of a failure.

But nobody else smiled. The rest of them shook their heads. "No," said Kenneth. "There isn't any need for you to lose your shirt, just because the rest of us are going to. Besides, twenty thousand isn't enough. We've got another ten thousand due in thirty days."

"I can raise ten thousand. I think I can anyway."

"But, Jim," spoke up Arnold Houghton, "that isn't the point, is it? If they're closing in on us, they're going to want every payment as soon as it comes due; and even if we get into production, on the saw, we aren't going to take in money that fast. We can't. It'll take six months before we see any real money."

James King looked at Susan again. Her smile was almost gone, but she was still hopeful.

"Can you get that saw on the line in thirty days?" he asked harshly, like an executive who had taken charge.

"Yes," said Kenneth, "but——"

"No 'buts.' I'm going to buy you thirty days. After that thirty days, I'm going to sweat and scream and come up with something to keep off the wolves. Are you going to let me in?"

There was no question. He drove them from the office and picked up the telephone. "New York City," he said, "Mr. Raymond Hornsby, Jefferson National Bank. I'll hold on."

Susan sat beside him while he bought the thirty days.

In the week that followed, it seemed as though a factory which had been humming before was twice as active and twice as consecrated. James had little office work to do. His main problem was to decide what to do when the thirty days were up. He was realist enough to know there was no easy solution. He searched in his mind and he searched in the eyes of Susan Kendall and he searched in the shops that housed the devoted employees of Maspreth Motors.

He searched, but he did not find. He found understanding, though, and he found comradeship. The men knew that he was the one who had at least temporarily saved their jobs. They let him know they knew. They took him as a friend, even to the extent of letting him sit grandly in the Maspreth Special Six when they opened the big glass case to do their weekly polishing one lunch hour.

"Like to hear it run?" asked the foreman.

"Gosh, yes. Will it?"

"Sure. We run it once, twice, maybe three times a year. I'll tell you what. We'll get it out and water the radiator, and you take it for a little ride this afternoon."

"I wouldn't want to do that."

"Why not? You won't hurt it. We ran it all over town last Fourth of July parade. Go ahead. Hey, Ben, get the ramp. Mr. King's going to do the town."

They eased it from the case. They put water in the radiator and checked the oil. They poured some gasoline into the tank and brought an old battery from some hiding place. The Maspreth fired at once, and the foreman throttled it down and climbed from the seat. "Take it away," he said.

James took it away. He sat on the smooth leather and he handled the crafted wooden steering wheel like the beautiful thing it was. He drove proudly up the company street to the office and honked the horn. Susan came running out to join him in his glory.

As he passed slowly through town, he found he had more friends than any man had a right to have. Merchants leaned from their doorways and waved. Small boys ran alongside and cheered. The policeman, parked at the intersection to watch for speeders, left his car to wave the Maspreth out onto the main highway.

He drove along the riverbank, exulting in the throb of the old engine. The top was down, and the wind whipped past, sending Susan's hair out behind in an amber cloud. He thought he had never been so happy.

He swung around in a farmer's driveway about five miles up the valley and headed back to town. As he neared the policeman's car again, he noted a strange growling noise from behind the car, but he was so absorbed in the passion of his progress that he did not let it bother him until it was a full-fledged grind. Then, horrified, he stopped.

The Maspreth came back to the factory pulled backward behind the tow truck from the Crossroads Garage. The big

foreman clucked in sympathy, crawled under the car and reported his findings.

"Someone drained all the oil out of the transmission and the rear end," he said. "The plugs are gone. That figures. The gears are probably all burred in one or the other, maybe both. Don't worry about it."

"Don't worry? When I've ruined this car that you've kept for nearly forty years?"

"Heck, you haven't ruined anything. We've got more rear ends and transmissions than you can shake a stick at. We'll have you out in it again by this time tomorrow. A couple of the boys will stay down tonight and change over. We can put in a whole new assembly if we want—drive shaft, wheels and all."

"You've got spare parts?"

The foreman laughed. "Spare parts? We've got spare cars. We've got a whole building full of pieces of these things."

Something clicked in James King's mind. "Wait a minute," he said. "Give it to me slowly. How many pieces for how many cars?"

"I don't know. Come and see."

The foreman led the way to a barnlike building adjacent to the generator-assembly shop. Inside was an accumulation that made James gasp. He grabbed Susan by the arm and headed her for the office.

"Have you got the inventory sheets where you can get at them easily," he asked her. "I'd like to see the whole batch."

She brought them, wondering, and he fumbled furiously. Then he straightened up and laughed. He grabbed her again, but this time it was to hold her close.

"Susan," he said, "I've found it. We've got it made. Susan, do you still want me to stay here and make it run?" He didn't wait for an answer. He kissed her hard. "Get the brass of this outfit in here, will you?" he said. "I think they'd like to hear this right away. And, while I'm talking to them. . . . " He gave her instructions.

A few minutes later, seated at a table with Kenneth Kendall, Arnold Houghton and the others, he read slowly from an old list in front of him.

"Two hundred and seventy-five frame assemblies, one hundred and thirty-eight closed bodies, one hundred and fifteen open bodies, one hundred and ninety-two assembled motors, nine hundred and five wheels, seats, steering assemblies, universals. Do you know what you boys have in stock?"

They shook their heads. "I'm not sure either. Susan's calling. I'll know in a minute. But I have to ask you this. Are you still going to need a finance man in your organization if it turns out that you've got finances enough to keep you going without any trouble until you get your saw in shape? I don't want to come in here under false pretenses. You might not need me any more at all."

"What are you talking about?" said Arnold Houghton. "We still have only your know-how between us and foreclosure."

"Maybe not," said James.

Susan came in and laid a slip on the table. He picked it up, and a big smile came over his face.

"Fifteen hundred to two thousand dollars," he said. "That's what you can get for a Maspreth Special Six. If you can make a hundred cars, you've got a backlog of a hundred and fifty thousand dollars right in that stock-shed. That's what I mean, Arnold. You don't really need me any more at all."

"Jim," said Kenneth Kendall. "We still don't know what you're talking about. What have we got a hundred and fifty thousand dollars' worth of? Old car parts?"

"Not old—antique. There's quite a difference, Ken. Susan's just called the biggest dealer in antique cars in New York City. He gave her this price. What else did he say, Susan?"

"He said old cars made of parts that had been in storage would be just as authentic as old cars that had been in storage complete. He said he'd be glad to handle just as many as you could make. He wants to be your distributor."

There was a momentary bedlam around the table. There was backslapping and handshaking. James King stood up. He tossed the inventory sheets to Arnold Houghton. Arnold Houghton tossed them back.

"Jim," he said, "you're a genius. There's just one trouble with you. You've been away too long. Do you really think we'd let you leave us now? Just try and get out of town—even for a weekend."

His eyes sparkled a little as he watched Susan reach out and take hold of James King's hand. "Well," he amended, "maybe for three or four days. Maybe for just long enough for a honeymoon." ■

The Supermen

George Summers was late in closing up. The Friday-night footfalls of the trading farmers had died away while he wiped the counter in his small lunchroom. It was a soft night with a small mist, and his motion was not hurried as he started for the door to snap the latch before his final act of cashing up.

There was a light shudder of brakes and the slam of a car door. He checked his movement toward the front, in anticipation of possible further business.

When the three young men strode in, he regretted his lateness and his waiting. They were of a type for whom he desired to do no favors, a breed that he feared because they were not of his age and he had given up trying to understand whatever he had read about them.

It was only through reading that he knew them for what they were. Center Brayton had never nurtured any such people. Center Brayton was too old in its fear of God and its stable employment. It had never felt the impact of the bursting of the disciplinary dam.

The three young men had an air of matured evil. They looked past the point of no return. There was no boyishness in their manner, no joy in their walk. They were not excited about the misty lateness in which they were abroad. They were not excited about anything.

Two of them walked in step toward the far corner by the register. One, tall and pimpled, flung a coarse-voiced summons at George.

"Cigarettes," he said.

George had a momentary ray of hope, and then he saw the third youngster reach over and snap the catch on the night latch and take up an indolent position where he could watch the street. After that, there was no more hope, and his spine tingled a little as he faced the two.

He stood and waited for them to declare themselves. That was all he could do. The telephone was too slow to be of use. The blows would be quicker. He never doubted the coming of the blows. He felt very tired.

The old wall clock ticked solidly, and the boy at the door shuffled his feet, grating the introdden sand.

George wondered what paralysis had gripped humanity that humanity had not been able to wipe out this creeping menace before it became a threat to the hinterlands around the city cradle.

George knew how vulnerable the hinterlands were. Center Brayton had never known hoodlums or crime even in the days of Dutch Schultz. It had been too small for even minor gangsters.

It was not too small for this new breed, these cold-faced, old-young spawn of neglected schools of vice. Nothing was too small for them, because the rewards of vice were not the reason for their acts. They sought only pain and savagery, and once they had discovered the weakness of the small towns, they would be back, again and again, menacing the streets even in their absence.

They were beginning to discover the small towns. An old man with an empty cash register and a ravished store had been found dead at Turner Corners just last week. The scouts were out from the cities, and it was going to take a strong shock to hold the evil to its old locale.

George noted the earmarks of the age, the long haircuts and the pseudo-Mexican sideburns, the black jacket on the one and the combat coat on the other. They showed no weapons even when they made their move. Their stance and their sneers seemed weapons enough. Their presence alone was a promise of violence.

"All right, man, this is it," suddenly said the tall invader. "You stand back against the wall and stay nice and still. You got things we want."

George backed up. He backed up tight against the shelves that lined the wall, the shelves packed with the familiar merchandise that had been his life since he had come home to find peace after the guns had gone quiet in Europe in 1945. He had gone a long way and seen much death to keep America from such as this. The thrust from abroad had been stopped, but the creed had seeped silently in.

He backed up tight to the shelves and he said nothing, but his soul cried out because he did not like what was coming. He resented the need, and he felt that, somewhere, there was much to be blamed.

"Hit the register, Joe," said the tall one.

The companion eased past George with a heedless push that seemed to have measured the actions to be expected from the merchant and to have found them wanting in hazard or even in bother. He punched the NO SALE key and the drawer opened wide. He scooped bills and change into his hand and so to his pockets.

"Sixty bucks, maybe," he stated.

The tall one spat on the floor. "Big deal," he said.

Joe brushed past George again, carelessly, as he had done before. He almost seemed to be inviting challenge, and George wondered if somewhere in the twists of his mind he needed some kind of justification for his already planned acts, some childish symbol like the knocking of a chip from a shoulder. George would have liked to explore the thought, but there was no longer time. Things seemed to be moving faster. The clock ticked again.

Joe had reached the end of the counter when the tall leader spoke once more.

"Wait a minute, Joe," he said. He turned his voice to George. "Where's the rest of it?"

"That's all there is," said George.

"Nuts."

He turned to the watcher at the door. "How's the street?" he asked.

"Quiet," said the watcher. "The whole town's asleep. Christ, what a burg."

"Tear the telephone, Joe," said the tall one.

Wires were snapped from the wall. The instrument was hurled across the room. The leader took a piece of lead pipe from his pocket.

"Hit him a couple, Joe," he said unemotionally. "He's got more dough than that."

Joe put his hand into his pocket and brought out a similar, unimaginative weapon. He slapped it into his other palm. He licked his lips and took a step along the counter toward where George stood, still backed against the shelves, one hand in front of him, the other resting in back for support.

George sighed. There was so much in living that was so hard to explain. There were so many sides to this thing that he wished he had time to consider them all, to weigh them, to moderate his needs, to offer mercy or opportunity or a guide to other paths. There wasn't time. These things had been tried by wiser men than he. These boys had probably been lectured to and prayed over and paroled and pleaded with.

He only wished he was sure that they were the probers who had done the job at Turner Corners.

Joe took another step.

"Why don't you just take what you have and leave?" asked George, his voice rising despite his weariness and his reluctant acceptance of their denial.

Again the clock was loud.

"Hurry up, Joe," said the tall one. "Do you need some help with the man?" He laughed, and in the stillness the laugh rang clear and brutal and cold.

That was when George, hating the need and the waste and the recrimination that he would launch tomorrow on the lacks that had forced this ugly end, brought up the hand that had rested behind him. It was typical of the stupid arrogance of the three hoodlums that they had not noticed this hand. It showed a lack in their education, a flaw in their quick course in crime, because in that hand was their undoing. The hand held a blue-steel Luger, and their overlooking it was an error that it was now too late to remedy and yet a natural error, because they had never before encountered any semblance of resistance in their pitiful victims.

It was a fitting weapon to confront them, because it was a relic of the days when hoodlumism in the black uniforms of the crooked cross had threatened the peace of the entire world. George had picked it up from the dead hand of a disillusioned superman.

For a moment, as Joe paused in midstride, as the tall one raised his arm for a savage throw, George thought idly of mere threats or words, but the hopelessness of any appeal save force was so clear to his inner being that he was discarding the thought even as he thumbed off the safety and ducked the flying pipe and squeezed the trigger. The Luger bucked once, and he swung it to the other near target and squeezed again. There was a gurgled something from Joe as he clutched at his belly and went down, but there was no sound from the tall one as he, in turn, collapsed.

The watcher at the door was yelling in full volume as he loosed the latch, but the gun spoke once more, and he grabbed his shoulder and raised the other arm aloft in surrender.

"Was it you boys at Turner Corners?" asked George, probing for the last remnant of defense, reaching for the denial that would serve to turn him from his task.

The boy nodded. He nodded twice, and then his face contorted and he opened his mouth to scream, and George set his lips and shot again, and the scream was cut off and the boy spun around and fell, face down, arms spread out like a fallen scarecrow, the fiery dragon on his coat stretched taut and strangely still.

Then the store was quiet except for the tick of the clock and the long-drawn sigh for the terrible need. ■

Please Respect the Residents

Bryan Judkins grew up with fear, with admonitions, with constant reminders of God's growing impatience with the acts of men, with knowledge of Satan's seductive power, with the outlining of penalties for lies and deceit.

Bryan's parents understood that God worked in mysterious ways. They accepted his gift of a child to raise, although in their middle age they had given up hope or expectation or even desire. They brought up Bryan in the way he should go, taking him with them to the "Church of the Rebirth." He learned about the blinding of the Syrians, about Elisha's mockers torn apart by bears, about the fires of Sodom and the demons sent to torture Eliphat.

God had favored Bryan's father in business and investment. Parental duty was clear. It was to win God's favor for Bryan. But Bryan was still only at the edge of favor when both parents died.

He was then ready for college. For two years he walked the plain path of liberal arts and seminary. Then, uneasy but nudged by math and science professors, he turned to engineering and design. His talent was obvious to his first employer. With the residue from his inheritance he bought an apartment in the city where he worked. He loved the city. He loved the brick and glass and chrome of the apartment. He found a church where all values were neutral. So was God.

It was in that church that he found Sara or Sara found him. Whoever found whom, there was a finding. There was marriage.

There were seven years of life together, years that Bryan was sure were all that a striving man had a right to expect.

The only problem was that he was afraid of Sara. She ruled him by his fear of losing her. She was adroit at giving and withholding, at pleasantry and disapproval. But his general contentment was too great to be disturbed by firmly announced decisions on parties or vacations or cars or changed desirability of friends. Only when her friends began easing out to the suburbs did Sara strike a real blow at contentment's base. Only then was he driven to fight.

"There's a house," said Sara, "that wasn't included in Ridgewood Acres. It's on the other side of a maple grove. The owner kept it but now she wants to sell."

"That's country," said Bryan. "Sara, you wouldn't like the country."

"I would. The city is stifling me. The suburbs would, too. Boxes in a patterned field, even though they're bigger now. Even though the lines waver. I've made an appointment with the owner. We're going Sunday."

"You never said that you wanted a house."

"I didn't. Now I do. Bryan, you're away all day. I'm here."

"Not much," he said, but he knew that this was touchy ground. He hurried to block response. "We'll go, but please don't plan so quickly. Let's think it over first. It's nice here. It's close to work. I like it."

"It's time to stretch out," said Sara. "The city sets up barriers."

"That's what I like," he ventured, but with no reason, no conviction, only prompted by some inner feeling that he knew could not be shared.

Still, there was a brief rebellion when they visited the house. It began as they drove under the maple branch arches of the approach lane to the Edwards house and the gabled structure came into sight. The three stories stretched up and out, rambling toward Victorianism, not quite reaching it, settling for Farmhouse Gothic.

"I don't want this damned place," he said. "It gives me the creeps just to look at it. Who's going to tend the grounds?"

"There's a service," Sara said. "We can afford it. We might get the house painted, too, although part of the appeal is in the grayness and the vines. At any rate, don't be difficult. We haven't seen inside."

"I know what it's like inside. We had houses like this on the outskirts of our town when I was a kid. Nobody lived in them. Nobody bought them. I don't know what happened to them. I suppose somebody tore them down. They were horrible houses."

"It wasn't easy then to modernize a kitchen," said Sara.

Martha Edwards answered Sara's knock. Martha, in what were close to costume clothes, looked older than the house and, like the house, displayed no frailty but rather an angular strength. She stood in the doorway, her eyes suggesting the mischief of youth as she inspected Bryan, definitely not Sara but Bryan, tilting her head, nodding finally when she spoke, deepening his apprehension.

"All right," she said. "I think you'll do. Respect is in you. Come in."

Bryan hung back as Sara stepped through the doorway. He looked at the brooding ridge behind the barn and at the small swampy pasture that he could already visualize as dotted with phosphorescence on misty nights of unease. He shivered.

"Respect for what?" he asked, but Mrs. Edwards didn't answer. She only smiled and in the smile was somehow contained the hint that she knew Bryan and knew Sara and knew more than Sara knew and more than Bryan wanted to remember.

"Sara," said Bryan, "this is not a house for you. This house is wrong."

She shrugged him off. "This house is made for me. Look at the size of the living room. It's almost a salon setting. Bryan, we're not in our old limits. This is better than Claire Newton's gathering room. She'll go home and turn green. Look, we can put the piano here and. . . . "

Bryan turned to Mrs. Edwards. "You wouldn't sell when they were laying out Ridgewood," he said. "Why are you selling now?"

"They would have torn it down. She won't. She likes a challenge."

"Oh, I do," said Sara. "And it is a challenge."

"Yes," said Mrs. Edwards, the smile not quite so certain then. "Yes, it is."

In the end, then, it was settled quickly but in the settling process lay the beginning of a strangeness in Bryan's mind that confused and frightened him. They moved in and the strangeness grew, a strangeness that was not caused by anything that happened but rather by something that seemed always to be on the verge of happening.

Sara's plans matured. There was more entertaining. There was more being entertained. Sara could rest in the mornings. Bryan could not. In him there grew fatigue. There also grew suspicion of the contentment that he once had felt, the thought that in it something must have been betrayed, the something vague. What he did know, positively, was that the after-work comfort of the city apartment eluded him in the Edwards house and that the house, like Sara, constantly held back part of itself. In the house, though, he was sure that the part held back was something he didn't want. He knew it was there, but he dreaded its revelation.

The revelation came, regardless of desire.

It came because the afternoon meetings of all the groups where Sara's daytime life was centered multiplied and naturally rotated in location. When Bryan came home to lights and cars leaving and Sara smiling in her knowledge of accomplishment, there was peace and warmth. When the house was empty, pending her return, Bryan sensed increasing chill.

Through the summer and early fall, he didn't mind. But when the beginnings of darkness edged closer and closer to the end of his working day, the shadows menaced him in the drive and the walk from the converted-barn garage seemed like a challenge thrown at the watchers who spied on him from behind the unlighted windows.

Bryan knew this was absurd, that there were no watchers, nothing in the house to menace him. But he could still feel the uncanny presence of the absurdities he denied and he remembered Mrs. Edwards's words about respect.

He had told himself, again and again, sometimes pretending that he believed his own words, that she meant respect for the wide pine floors or the tricky fireplaces in which the wood had to be laid just right to keep the smoke from going everywhere except up the chimney.

If she had meant the shadows and whatever it was that whispered when there was no wind, then how else could a person treat them except with respect? They lived in the dignity that their power demanded.

But there were no such things. There were no such things. He knew this. He didn't believe in shadows without substance.

Yet quick looks over his shoulder became routine. So did the concentration on the upper story of the building as he neared the front porch . . . to spot the expected movement of the curtains in the empty house.

There would be no movement. He was a fool. He was a man grown and he had lost the stupid fears of childhood. He had banished the dream horrors of trembling nights. He told himself that. He concentrated on the telling.

But there came an evening when he shut the front door behind him and looked up the stairs and knew that the banishment was only a pretense, that all he had done was to pull a curtain over truth, to mask it with thin veil, slowly woven and swiftly dissolved.

He stood in the hall. The last sunlight was coming through an upstairs window, a thin beam that had no power to muster the forces of happy brilliance but had been grasped as it was dying and turned into a tool of revelation.

The weakened glow was throwing the silhouette of the banisters on the hall wallpaper. Recognition chilled Bryan into complete immobility. An old familiarity gave him the clue.

He had seen that banister silhouette before, years before. When he was a boy, he had seen the wild shapes climb those stairs and disappear; seen the Edwards house in some translucent form all wreathed in a bank of mist that swept across the dawn horizon when his tense expectation of horror was almost over for one more night.

He knew the Edwards house. He knew it well. It was the refuge of the demons described to him in his youth by the aging parents to whom he had been born after thirty years of marriage had removed all chance of being wanted, being loved, or being understood.

The Edwards house was where the *things* came from when they started out to visit small boys in the night and punish their misdeeds. All through his life, Bryan had feared the *things* and now he had invaded their home.

He was held beside the door in rigid fear, unable to fight, unable to think, not daring to challenge the horror by turning on the light, yet not daring, either, to stand undefended in the growing dark.

Sara's rattling of the doorknob dissolved the rigidity and permitted him to move and snap the switch. He opened the door for her.

"Just got here," he said.

Even that small lie made him glance fearfully at the stairs. But the lie was necessary. This was a piece of knowledge that he couldn't reveal to Sara. She would have deep scorn for a memory that proved the presence of beings created from mist.

Bryan was very quiet for the rest of that evening.

He had seen the Edwards house when he was young because he had watched the distorted shadows head toward it. He had known, then, what the house was, because he had realized that it must exist. The *things* couldn't stay constantly in the homes of all their potential victims. They watched from a distance. They *came.*

Their coming was part of the pattern of prophecy. It wouldn't have been included had they been always at hand.

He could remember the exact words of his father.

"The woman with the twisted face will *come* and.... "

"The old man with the big teeth will *come* and.... "

But they didn't have to *come* to the Edwards house.

A man who lived in the Edwards house, the home of the twisted-faced or big-toothed but otherwise formless avengers of lies, deceit, and disobedience, was within easy reach.

He stopped fighting belief and accepted the fact that he was in deadly danger and that one false step would bring the end.

After the night of the banister silhouette, nothing dulled the knowledge. The beings became positive and arrogant.

They waited inside the chimney flues, radiating their presence. They lurked in the recesses of the cellar and in the corners of the attic. In their fluid and changeable form they seeped through walls to escape the light, but they waited, always, for the unwary to step over the line of wickedness and thus permit the perpetration of horrors.

In the nights, the house belonged completely to them. In the nights, they took charge. Bryan could sense them as he lay in the tension of terror. He knew that if he made one mistake important enough to be judged worthy of vengeance, he would be theirs, he and the house and the whole fluid world in which his mind had lately moved.

With his nervousness constantly growing, Bryan began his third year in the Edwards house. The year started on an overcast day in late November, a day made more dismal by the obvious death of the fragile stalks and stems and by the equally obvious withdrawal of the strong trees and bushes into hibernation.

It didn't feel like snow, but the clouds were heavy. It would be dark early. It was not yet five o'clock, but the lights were coming on in the houses. If Sara were not home, there would be a black blanket around the Edwards place.

There would be shuffling and soft sighs and currents of air when the front door was opened.

Bryan felt his gut contract in a mild spasm. On impulse, he turned into the Cranston doctor's parking lot. Office hours ended at five. The doctor should still be there and, with luck, not busy.

A visit to the doctor wouldn't hurt and the time thus taken might let Sara get home first if she had been out for the afternoon.

The doctor was more experimental than positive.

"You're building up a tolerance, maybe," he said. "We'll try Librex for a change from Librium. It might help. Been bothering you more than usual, has it?"

"I don't know about frequency," said Bryan. "It hits pretty often."

"Spastic colitis . . . just mental pressures. . . . Damn it, Bryan, we just don't know enough about mental pressure, mental power. If we could get control of the power in the human mind, we could eliminate all the evil in the world. Talk about moving mountains . . . we could *make* mountains. We could make whole worlds. We could put people on them . . . only who'd want to?"

"I guess my mental powers aren't too good, Doc."

"Nobody's are really good. But that's partially because we don't try. We don't practice. This is interesting, Bryan. Anybody—anybody at all—can hold off pains or a flow of agony or . . . Dammit, there've been actual cases of men who walked ten or twenty feet after they were shot through the heart."

"With enough mind control they could have walked fifty?"

"Maybe a mile. Anybody can hold off things for a while. With practice he can hold off longer and longer. . . . Hell, I'm due to eat with Dennis and then start house calls. Get out of here."

Outside again, Bryan checked his watch. Good, he'd used up a half hour. That was all he'd done. Librium or Librex or Liberace . . . that didn't matter. For four months the nights would be longer than the days. That mattered. It was the night that mattered.

The other side of the barn was empty when he parked his Ford. The delay hadn't helped a bit. Sara wasn't home. It seemed as though she was never home lately . . . not soon enough, anyway, to turn on the lights.

Bryan let himself in the front door, listening for the latch to click behind him. He stood in the hall for a minute with his eyes shut, but that didn't help and couldn't help. A man couldn't stay in the hall and, even if he did, the hall was open to attack from three directions.

But that was stupid thinking, too. Open doorways or closed doorways, walls or lack of walls didn't matter. If this enemy had reason to attack, a bank vault wouldn't be a barrier.

Treat them with respect. Treat them with respect. Well, he'd been doing that. One way was to avoid startling them, to let them know you were coming so that they could slide out of sight without offending or being offended.

He stamped his feet, took a deep breath, and shouted, "I'm here. I'm home. I'm putting on the lights."

He didn't expect a verbal answer. Why should they answer? They were watchers, not welcomers. Of course they wouldn't answer.

But a damp air current brushed his cheek. There were creaking noises near the stairs. There was a momentary smell of mustiness, like that of a suitcase long stored in the cellar.

The wide arch to the living room was on Bryan's left. The stairs were directly in front of him. The old dining room, now the library, was on the right. He lighted the hall first, then the dining room, then moved through the living room, flipping switches as he went.

That was what he needed, light. Light helped more than Librex. Light brought temporary peace. It might not save a man from execution of a sentence passed in council, but it could be a protection against the impulsive actions of a loner.

Bryan was pouring the whiskey when he heard Sara drive past the house to the barn. He found another glass and poured more.

"Hi," she said from the doorway. "I meant to be here. . . . "

Sara was carrying a package, big, square, but thin.

"What's in there?" he asked.

"A picture. I'll show you. Did you fix me a drink? Wait until I come down. I went to a gallery and I'm afraid I splurged."

She started up the stairs. Bryan carried the picture in his left hand and his drink in his right as he walked into the living room and sat down.

Sara went to the kitchen before she joined him. The freezer door opened and closed. The stove switches snapped. Water ran, a pan rattled, paper crackled.

In less than five minutes she had the food preparation under way and was sampling her drink. Then she put it down and picked up the wrapped picture.

"It got to me," she said. "I'm furious at myself, but I just had to have it. It's a Leonard Bleuve. It's abstract."

She ripped through the small tabs of tape. The wrapping fell to the floor and Sara held up the picture for Bryan to see.

"Dear God," he said.

Coldness closed in from four directions. A shaking started in his lower jaw and worked toward his neck chords. He swallowed and struggled and, in the process, he spoke again but he had no idea of what he said. His speech was not a statement. It was a plea from the edge of an abyss.

Sara heard him. She answered with defensive viciousness.

"Do I know whose picture it is?" she said. "Is that supposed to be funny? It's abstract art. It's a poem in paint. Its beauty is in its being. Whose picture! Bryan, you're hopeless."

The cold air moved away. Bryan managed to get his glass to his lips. When he had gulped, he spoke, and this time he heard what he said.

"Take it back."

It was the first direct and positive order that he had ever given Sara in the years they had spent together.

"What did you say?" she asked.

"I won't have it," he shouted. "I won't have it in the house. Don't you see what it is? Are you insane? Take it back."

He turned his eyes away from the picture and stared directly into the full gleam of the floor lamp. What was going on? How could any artist reproduce so perfectly one of the creatures that slid silently from shadow to shadow?

No painter could have a mental image . . . certainly not a material model of . . . but there it was, all eyes and arms and clutching hands and an outline clearly drawn yet blending into its background.

The floor lamp was not bright enough to blur Bryan's vision in the way he wanted it blurred. He stared at the picture again, conscious of Sara's stormy protest against his shouting and his defiance but unable to concentrate on her words because another thought was nudging its way into his mental storm and he needed time to reach for clarity.

"Sara," he said. "Just shut up for a minute. Shut up."

Never before had he said such a thing and her response was given in absolute fury, but he was not bothered by it because the new thought had jolted its way into a center of understanding.

He had the answer. Some outlander, some *thing* that was born in the same savage world as the settled residents of the Edwards house but was a part of a feuding rival culture, had chosen this way of invading. It had become part of a canvas, hoping to set up an invasion bridgehead unobserved.

Bryan had too much confidence in the Edwards house occupants to think the outlander had any chance of success. It would be destroyed. But what would happen to the person who seemed to be aiding this doomed attempt at intrusion?

Sara was screaming. Bryan cut through her anger with a flat firm statement.

"Hand me that thing," he said. "I'm going to burn it."

As he spoke, there was a low growl that seemed sourceless. There was a tingling on Bryan's scalp. There was a movement on the canvas, a flicker that Bryan barely saw but that he knew had changed something. Was a hand in a different position?

There. There it was again. This time he identified it. The vague, multi-colored shape had eased away from the background. The movement was one of tension, of tightening muscles, of preparation for attack.

Bryan gripped his chair arm. The dryness of his mouth denied the possibility of what he was positive had been a recent wetting. There was no moisture on his tongue as he licked his lips.

Sara had stopped talking. She was looking at him with a puzzlement that proved she was past attack, past recrimination, groping for an explanation that would satisfy her logical modern mind.

"Are you sick, Bryan?" she asked.

"No. I'm just trying to help you."

"Nonsense."

"Sara, that's an intruder. They won't want it here. They have a right to choose who comes. Don't you understand that?"

"Bryan, you're babbling."

He was relaxed, then, almost to a point of formlessness. He was detached, too, like an observer. That was as it should be . . . as it should have been. He was not the object of the watchfulness of the creatures which roamed in the night.

He had been watching them while they watched.

That was when he laughed. The laughter was as intense as the fear it replaced. The laughter was uncontrollable. He knew that and he made no effort at control. He laughed until the laughter spent itself.

When he spoke, his voice was firm. "Sara," he said, "who gave you that picture?"

She sensed the sureness of the knowledge, but she challenged the sensing and the sureness. She was facing the unexpected, but she fought.

"Nobody gave me anything. I bought it with my bridge winnings. Bryan, what's the matter with you?"

"Nothing. Be careful, Sara. Please be careful. I'll try to help you, but you have to tell me the truth."

"Help me? Help me with what? Bryan, you're having flashes of fever or something. I'm going to call the doctor."

"Sit still," he said. "I've just come from the doctor's. He talked about . . . Sara, that's it . . . the power! Please. I *will* help you. I can hold them off long enough to start. We start with the truth. Who gave it to you?"

"I bought it."

"Stop lying. It came from some man. Who? Who's the man, Sara? Who's been in arrears and made a payment of . . . well, I'll have to guess at that . . . five hundred dollars? No, not enough. Bleuve . . . I never heard of Bleuve, so he's probably newly discovered and riding high. Was it a payment of a thousand dollars, Sara?"

She took a long drink. "I don't have any idea what you're talking about," she said, "and I don't like being called a liar."

"Get rid of that picture. You're in peril, deadly peril. God, I don't have any idea. . . . Sara, tell the truth. Who got a thousand dollars worth of . . . shall we say, companionship?"

"You bastard. You suspicious bastard. You've gone crazy."

"Sara, I don't give a damn, actually . . . not any more. I don't care who or where or when. You and I have had it. We're through. But don't let *them* at you, Sara. Save yourself. Tell the truth. Who was it?"

"Are you really accusing me of what I think you are?"

"Yes. Don't play games. . . . "

She finished her drink and stood up. "You're out of your mind," she said. "I'm going upstairs and call the doctor. I'm afraid to stay in the same room with you."

"You're making a mistake," he said.

"And I'm locking my bedroom door."

"That won't help."

She carried the picture as she started for the stairs. He shuddered. He shouted.

"Don't take that, Sara. Leave it here."

"For you to ruin? I will not. I paid for it. It's my picture. I'll take it where I want."

"Please . . . "

"Go to Hell," she said.

She rounded the stairway turn. He heard the door slam and the key click the lock.

Bryan went out to the kitchen and turned off the switches on the stove. He opened the porch door and took a deep breath. Then he went back to the living room, put the whiskey within reach and sat there, concentrating intently but quietly.

In the house there was no movement that Bryan's ears could catalog as movement. There was no life in the air.

He put his mind on the picture, thinking determinedly, becoming more and more intense.

Stay away from her, he thought. Stay back. Leave her alone. Dammit, she doesn't *realize*. . . .

He could sense the passage of his commands out into the room. He could trace the waves of thought. He was holding a barrier against pressing forces which were trying to close in.

He felt his temples throbbing and then he caught a feeling of slackness in the pressure, an acknowledgment of fortifications found too strong.

His eyes were almost closed. His jaw was set. He willed himself to prove defiance, to fight for Sara harder than he would have fought to save himself, and that was strange, too, because he knew dimly that Sara could no longer share his world. But he added to his tenseness. The pressures eased some more.

He relaxed for the moment it took to fill his lungs and set himself in tension once again.

Too late, he knew his error. The lull had been a trap. Violence set the air currents in a turmoil. He was caught in relaxation when he heard the scream.

It was sharp and loud, but it ended while its volume was still increasing. It was cut off quickly, with the finality of a slammed drawer.

Bryan started to rise, but he knew there was no use and no need. He settled back, sighed, and poured a fresh drink, noting the subtle renewal of the small sounds and the whisper of shadows passing.

A newfound friendly warmth seeped up from the cellar through the cracks in the old, old boards. A promise, possibly, of friendship and protection for a respectful host to the resident unknown. ■

Confusing the Issue

Pomish Landing on Lake Glorianna in the Adirondacks was one of those towns that divided people into two classes, natives and non-natives. Non-natives were kept outside of a social stockade.

Pomish Landing was a resort town. At both approaches there were big signs that said, "Welcome Stranger." But that applied only to strangers who were willing to spend their money fast and get out.

Carl Carmer described Pomish Landing when he described the Adirondack villages in general as being settled by necessity rather than by desire. He said the original inhabitants were Maine and New Hampshire and Vermont men who tried to migrate to the rich Ohio lands by going straight west. They became bewildered in the mountains, gave up trying, and raised sons whose descendants have been bewildered ever since.

Pomish certainly wasn't the kind of town for Doctor Armstrong, a retired history professor, to try to change. He did try. He had partial success. He didn't change the town but the town did change him.

At his second town meeting, Dr. Armstrong suggested that it might be a good idea to do something about all the junk cars that grew and multiplied in the side yards all over town. He found the vague, rubbery, non-opposing opposition that characterizes such societies.

Arnold Hurley said he needed his old cars because he never knew when a Chevy transmission might come in handy. The next speaker, Joe Kellogg, said that a Chevy never amounted to a hoot when put to a good load. Pete Russell said his father had a horse that won a blue ribbon at Rutland.

The moderator ruled the discussion out of order and went on to the next business without bothering to take a vote.

A week or so after that, Dr. Armstrong stopped me as I was leaving the store. He said, "Listen, I like this town and I don't want to try to run it or anything but I do wish I could just say something once in a while without being so solidly squelched."

"Confusion is the key," I said. "At least that's the only key I know. What I do is to reach back into some town where I lived before and get a story about some old guy. When I tell the story, they think I'm talking about their grandfather because he would have done the same kind of thing. So they think I must be related to somebody and that gives me a permit to make little suggestions."

"Well," he said, "in this town I guess it's easy to get confused. I'm pretty confused right now."

"That's progress. You can be a native anyplace if you're confused enough. Work at it."

"Thank you," said Dr. Armstrong. "I'll give it a try."

At the next town meeting, he got his opening and he dove for it. The man from New Jersey who had purchased the drug store spoke up and suggested that, under "any other business," the town should consider hiring a life guard for the public beach.

Pete Russell said he didn't know anybody he wanted to save. Ned Bennett said his father knew a man who drowned in the bathtub. Arnold Hurley said he wished he knew where he could buy a used bathtub cheap. Joe Kellogg announced that women's bathing suits were getting too scanty and there ought to be a law.

So Dr. Armstrong stood up and moved that the meeting adjourn before everybody died of thirst instead of drowning.

On the way out, Pete Russell came over to him and said, "Stop in at the Landing Lights with us, Professor. I'm buying."

Strength from the Hills

I had a hole in my belly and it hurt. I had pieces cut out and edges trimmed back and stitches made neatly to hold me together.

There was no water for days and days.

The first day I thought about orange juice or ginger ale. I thought about coffee or tea or maybe a malted milk.

The rest of the days I thought about water.

I thought about mountain springs and deep wells bored through the dry rock until the spouting veins were reached. I thought about rivers full of water and brooks with little springs feeding them along shaded banks. I thought about mossy stones by seeping rivulets.

I remembered a stream that rushed down a mountain near a spot where I used to load fieldstone on a truck. Every day I would stop and lie down and wash my face and drink and then I would take off my shoes and sit with my hot and tired feet in the stream.

I lay there in bed and I would have given all my hopes for almost everything I had ever wanted in return for a never ending drink out of a sweet glistening pipe stuck in the side of a hill to draw the water from a flowing vein to the attention of travelling man.

My tissues were parched and my throat was dry. There was a tube in my stomach to suck up even the moisture that fed feebly from drying muscles and dehydrated organs.

I was thirsty enough to need five minutes alone with a boiling spring before I reached the point where I could get any water through to my throat.

I started making an inventory of all the springs I had passed in my life, passed casually without any more than a brief flicker of recognition. I thought of springs covered with leaves in the hardwood growths. I thought about springs on the edges of fields, springs with little pockets of moving sand on their bottoms where the clear pure water from down below was pushing aside the obstacles to its emergence.

I thought about dug out and wooden boxed springs, down overgrown paths from decaying cabins, springs which flowed through widening crevices in mossy, rotting boards, but which were still sweet to smell and icy delicious to taste.

I thought about the pipe stuck in the bank along the road beside the upper Kennebec, the pipe which flowed day and night, winter and summer, wet weather or dry, with the strength from the forested hills.

I was very thirsty, yet I knew that pipe ran full. I knew that buckets of water, tubs of water, barrels of water, flowed from that pipe while I needed but one cupful to make me happy and glad.

But of course I needed more than a cupful. I needed a barrel brim full to the cooper's hoop.

I didn't get any water. I got tubes poked in my veins and I got bottles full of yellow liquid and red liquid and white liquid pumped in my veins.

I didn't get any water for what seemed a year. Then I got a spoonful and another spoonful. I got a mockery of moisture and my soul cried out and I knew that never again would I pass a pipe in the road without taking a long, long, drink.

I didn't keep the vow, of course, when I was on my feet again. I grew careless and I passed the springs with the casual look, the hesitation, the neglect.

Today, though, I saw the spring by the side of the road by the upper Kennebec and I stopped and looked and walked reverently over and drank.

I remembered the hospital. I took a big cupful and another cupful and another.

I partook of the strength of the hills for I need their strength. I need their waters within me, water filled with iron and copper and potassium and lime and all the other elements of the good Maine land.

I filled my cup and I drank to the hills and all the old need came back. I drank to the dryness of the past. I drank until I could drink no more.

And the water from the hillside came rushing still through the pipe, water enough for many men, for many years.

Water enough for me and for my sons and for yours.   ■

Union Station Remembered

It was a long time ago, when seventy-two hours was a gift from the gods, especially if seventy-two suddenly became a hundred and twenty, due to the wandering hand of an officer who had dated the liberty to start on what he thought was the same day but which was really forty-eight hours later. That's a little hard to understand, but understanding isn't really needed. The big point was that, although there were repairs to be made in a shipyard at Yonkers, we weren't supposed to have any liberty at all. I had sent for Dottie to come to New York. Then the navy changed its mind. I spoke up for taking a quick trip to Maine to see my boys.

Dottie and I piled on the old State of Maine special which left New York at about nine o'clock, wandered around Massachusetts and New Hampshire for twelve hours or so, and ended up at Union Station. It made a long night but, in those days, people were hanging onto the rear platform and sitting on suitcases in the aisles. Everyone was congenial. People sang and ate fluffy sandwiches and borrowed cigarettes and slept and played cards and formed a little world of their own.

Union Station was also a little world, a world of light and heat and food and drink and announcements of trains leaving and coming. It was full of couples kissing each other goodbye or kissing each other hello. There must have been ten children running around shining shoes, and lines by every ticket window. It was a quiet place. It had a lot of life to be so soon dead.

We had three hours or so to wait for the next train to Waterville. We wandered upstreet, not paying much attention, living for the moment, because there aren't many moments in a hundred and twenty hours. We didn't know much about Portland. We didn't need to.

In a record store a girl reached under the counter and came up with three Bing Crosby records that she had saved from the civilians. As we stood looking in a window in a candy store, a man came running out with a half pound box and gave it to Dottie. "Just from me," he said, "a nothing, just from me."

We had a cup of coffee and the countergirl wouldn't let us pay. We found that a variety store just happened to have a couple of pairs of nylons in Dottie's size.

If we had had three days to spend in Portland, instead of three hours, we would have had to hire a box car.

That's really all there is to the story. We got home and we were happy for a few days and then I got another train and walked up the gangway with just fifteen minutes to spare.

The curse of a good memory is that things like these do not take on a misty air of unreality as time goes by. They remain sharp and vivid and poignant. They are as clear as the conversation of last night. Sometimes they hurt.

When I drive past the silence and the debris and the blankness of Union Station, I can still remember it as it was during its brief resurgence of pride in the years of the war. The grief that was stoically held in check or hysterically released in Union Station, added to that which was present in a thousand such stations all over the country, was a measure of the days of our glory.

No matter what happens to us in the future, Union Station will have no part to play. It saw a lot of life. It will see no more. It is dead. It had to go to make way for progress. No city can stand still, and movement is the destroyer of ghosts.

But I am glad that I can still shut my eyes if I want to, and feel the sway of a passenger train, smell the singular odor of a railroad car, hear the whistle blow proudly for the lonesome crossings, note the tick, tick, tick of the wheels on the rails. I am glad that I can remember Union Station, taste the individual chicken pies that the lunchroom used to feature, think of the quiet movement of the mail trucks on the big platform, smell the confined smoke of the old soft coal.

I am glad that I didn't miss that. I am going to miss a lot of things like trips to far stars and perhaps a tunnel under the ocean, but I didn't miss Union Station, and maybe Union Station was more romantic than the things that are yet to come.　■

A Boy is Lost

I stepped up to the ticket window, put down my money, said, "Two adults and two children, please."

The girl looked at me a little strangely. Jody stepped up beside me and said, "Dad, not any more."

That was the way I first realized that they had grown up. It might not have happened so suddenly if we had been in the habit of movie going at regular intervals. We weren't. The nearest theater was fifteen miles away. In the summer, spring, and fall we were too busy to go. In the winter it always seemed like a long cold haul home.

In one of those gaps when we were untouched by Hollywood, both boys passed the twelve-year-old differential.

I didn't say anything more at the theater, but I made up my mind that I'd have to start enjoying those boys a little more seriously because time was getting short.

Good intentions have a certain moral value but they have a way of remaining intentions. One thing came up, then another. The next thing I remember was putting Jody on a bus for Cornell. My woodworking shop had burned. I was running a bulldozer over at Lee, Massachusetts, but I was home for the weekend.

"Do you like your job?" he asked me as we waited for the bus.

"No," I said, "nobody does anything. I could do as much with a power shovel, two trucks, and a farm crawler as that crew is doing with a half million dollars worth of equipment."

He didn't say any more until he got on the bus. Then he turned. I thought he was going to say goodbye. He didn't.

"Why don't you quit and take Joel fishing?" he said.

He was seventeen years old. He was smarter than I was. He was right. He smiled, then, and I lost him. I didn't know that I had lost him, of course. I thought he'd be coming home, now and again, for four years, and then I guess I figured he'd build a house next door or something. A man doesn't look ahead and consciously plan for the time when he won't have his boys any more. The knowledge that they are gone drifts in slowly, against the will to change the decision.

It is only when a boy is gone for a year, two years, three years, five years, that the fact becomes established. Then come the thoughts of what better uses should have been made of the time that there was. These thoughts are not comforting because they reveal thoughtlessness, selfishness, obsessions with the practical, and the misconception that time will stand still.

Dreams drift in, dreams that once were reality.

"I want to work with you on the windows."

"You'd help a lot more if you'd take that pile of stay lath and drive the nails out of it."

"Couldn't we take a lunch tonight and go down by the river and eat?"

"A man is coming to see me about building a cottage."

The stay lath could have waited. The man and I didn't do any business. He wanted a ten thousand dollar house for thirty-five hundred.

So there was a lot undone when Jody stepped on that bus. It was too late to do it. The time had passed. There was still Joel, however. There is still Joel. With Joel I have been granted a reprieve. Although he is on his own, learning his trade, developing his skills, he lives at home. Maybe this is to make up for the time we lost long ago.

Joel wasn't recognizing very much by the time I enlisted. When I got home, he was three-and-a-half years old and he hadn't had any experience with fathers coming on the scene to upset what he considered a normal existence. He didn't accept me for over a year. He was interested, but wary. He liked to ride but he never asked me. He didn't speak to me at all. He went to his mother and asked her if she would ask me if he could go. Then, even if we were gone four hours, he would just sit silently on the seat.

I mogged this up, too. I could have gotten to him a lot sooner if I had known how.

Regrets bake no bread. The only thing is, they are hard to stifle. If there were time enough in life to make up for mistakes it would be different. There isn't time. Even though a single night or even an hour may seem like an eternity, life itself is just a breath, a single shaft of light between two dark patches of the unknown. ■

Adventure on Route One

There is no mundane meandering to follow here. This is the
description of modern adventure. Some people think that
adventure is dead, that D'Artagnan was one of the last men to
find adventure on the road, in the fields, and in the city streets.
They are wrong.

Adventure still lurks. Traps still wait for the unwary.

On the day I had my adventure, I had been to Portland to
partake of the nauseating pap that is doled out to summer
schooling teachers. I had sat through this nonsense and I was
on my way home. I was filled to the brim with social welfare
statistics which I was duty bound to retain for the summer and
which I would then be put to the inconvenience of banishing
from my mind.

I was surly. I hated people. I especially hated the driver who
passed me at a light on Congress Street just because I sat for
awhile after it turned green so that I could watch a pretty girl
turn a windy corner.

Then I ran into my adventure. I got catalogued. Right in front
of me loomed a big sign that said, "Slow—Traffic Survey."
There was a policeman beside the sign to inspire respect in
folks who couldn't read. He motioned me to bear to the right
into a roped off alley behind a couple of other cars.

I bore.

I find that it is expedient to bear right or left as people in
uniforms motion you to do. It saves a lot of explanations.

112

In this case, it didn't save any at all. I had just entered the alley when a man clambered half in my window, right next to my face. He had a clipboard with a lot of forms on it.

"Where from?" he said.

"Portland," I said.

"Where are you going?"

"Home."

He paused for a minute. He looked me over. I knew that something was wrong. It was.

"You're going the wrong way," he said.

"No, I'm not. I'm going home. I live in Kennebunkport and Kennebunkport is right down this road twenty-five minutes, turn left where I turn left, and then on until you get to the ocean."

"I know where Kennebunkport is," he said.

"Oh?"

"You said you were from Portland."

"I just came from there."

"That isn't what I asked. Oh, never mind. You're from Kennebunkport and now you've been in Portland?"

"Yes. I'm going home and have lunch and. . . . "

This process was evidently supposed to take much less time because the road ahead was empty and my man looked grim.

"Never mind," he said. "Never mind."

"Is that all?" I asked.

"Yes. That's more than all."

"Good-bye," I said. I started forward. He came running alongside me. I stopped.

"Was there something else?" I inquired.

"Yes. I want to get loose from your door handle. I'm caught."

"You're also squeezing my cigarette, but never mind. It was almost all smoked anyway."

It was then that I saw the wisp of smoke.

"My cigarette is down inside your shirt," I told him.

He thrust himself fiercely away. There was a brown hole where everything had been white before. He commenced beating at himself. He pulled his shirt tail out, right there in public. He let the butt fall to the pavement.

"It's all right," I said. "I've got more."

I left him, then. I was afraid he'd want to apologize and he didn't need to. He couldn't help it because I smoke with my outside hand.

If they put those barricades up again, I'll try to do better. I like to help make statistics. I like to be counted. I like to brighten the day for the poor public servants who must get terribly tired dealing with people who are dopes. ■

Computer Collections

On the fifth day of every month I receive my regular note from the Blank Book Company. Inside the note is a yellow slip. I have been receiving these for twenty-two months now, so I do not need to read them. I know what they say.

The note is simply a credit memo. Two years ago, I bought a book directly from these publishers. I wasn't sure of the price so I sent six dollars. The price, plus tax and mailing cost, totalled $4.16. So the credit memo is for $1.84.

Rubber stamped on the memo is this admonition: "DO NOT REMIT. THIS IS A CREDIT BALANCE."

But on the yellow slip which is always in the same envelope, are pleading words with a different import. The slip says, "PLEASE. Our accounts are not permitted to be in such prolonged arrears. Won't you send your money and save your credit standing? If there is any question about the amount you owe us, won't you let us know?"

I don't have any question, so I have never let them know. After telling me twenty-two times that they owe me a dollar and eighty-four cents, they shouldn't have any question either.

But there must be a question somewhere.

Last month I pondered the ethics of the situation and I wrote to my confused friends. It wasn't easy to compose the letter. I could foresee difficulties. These companies are rather impersonal and I wasn't sure that the Blank Book Company would appreciate the humor of a situation where they had been dunning me for an amount which they owed me and which they quite properly kept telling me not to send.

But the difficulties had to be dared. Twenty-two reminders about the dangers to my credit rating if I did not send the money that they didn't want because I didn't owe it ... twenty-two letters at five cents each ... a dollar and ten cents was already spent out of the dollar eighty-four that seemed to be the cause of the pain.

So I tried. I wrote.

"Dear Friends: In regard to the $1.84 which is outstanding on your books, I would suggest that you replace the monthly announcements about its presence with one final letter containing your check to me. I know that this would be a revolutionary approach, but think of the advantages. Not only would my page in your ledger be clean and waiting for new business, but you would no longer have to dun me for what you owe me."

In a week I got the answer. It was brief and hopeful.

"Dear Mr. Clark: Thank you for your letter. We all know that there are times when circumstances make it difficult to meet one's current obligations. We are turning your suggestion over to our credit manager. You will hear from him."

I did hear from him, but he was less kind.

"Dear Mr. Clark: It seems to us that this is such a small sum that there should be no real problem about its payment. I am sending a statement in case you have misplaced your last one."

The statement was there, too. It said, "Cr. $1.84." It was rubber stamped, "Do not remit. This is a credit balance."

That put another fifteen cents in the kitty, ten from the company and five from me. I gambled a nickel more.

"Dear Blank Company: Do me a favor. Unplug your accounting machine for five minutes and let a bookkeeper look at my card. I think that will correct the confusion."

This time the answer took two weeks.

"Dear Mr. Clark: There is no chance of a misunderstanding. Your account is correct as enclosed. Please give it your attention."

The letter was right. The account was correct. The account was, "Cr. $1.84 ... DO NOT REMIT."

I followed instructions. I gave it my attention. I gave it some thought. Finally, fearful that the local credit bureau was frenziedly downgrading me to a "D" rating because of a national report that I was nearly two years in arrears to the Blank Book Company, I sent the company my check for $1.84.

But the machines are not that easily fooled. Yesterday, I had my answer. It was terse. It said, "Please. Our accounts are not permitted ... statement enclosed ... save your credit standing."

And the statement said, "Cr. $3.68. DO NOT REMIT. THIS IS A CREDIT BALANCE." ■

Old Stupid Cat

Old stupid cat started his winter wariness away back in September. We had a chilly evening. When he went to start on his summer scheduled nocturnal tour, he was greeted by a slight drop in temperature as the door was opened. He stopped and shook his whole front half. He lifted one leg and shook it even harder. Then he turned and looked up with a scowl that would have discouraged even a phony oil stock salesman.

"My soul," said Dottie, "are you going to start that already?"

The cat didn't answer. He disdains to make explanations. He merely went back inside and lay down on the rug.

But that was the pattern. That was the plot. It takes the decrepit dope about two hours to get outside in the morning and about four hours at night. He makes about seven or eight tries each time before he finally probes so close to the doorsill that an alert door opener can scoop him up quickly with a gentle foot under the cat's chest and send him surging the rest of the way.

Meanwhile he keeps somebody jumping up and down because his passes at the door seem to have immediacy. He rushes over and stands. He looks back at the audience. Then when someone opens the door, the cat jumps back, skirts his servant, and rounds the corner into the kitchen. He isn't hungry but he would rather eat than go out.

I never saw a cat before with such a paunch. His boredom makes him eat, not his appetite. He sleeps awhile, wakes up, thinks it is morning, and wants his breakfast. Some nights he eats breakfast five times.

118

Now I don't have the kind of patience that a cat lover should have. I know that, if this were a young cat, I would open the door once and the cat would go out, voluntarily or with help. But this cat is not young. I refrain from violence. There are two reasons.

The first reason is physical. A man might just as well try to stop a mill saw by grabbing a tooth. But heavy gloves would remedy that. I have gloves.

But I also have a certain sympathy. That's hard to explain. I don't like cats. If I did like cats, this one would be the exception. The vicissitudes of living, however, have made us sharers of a certain bond. Old cat has not lived a spotless life. Neither have I. Old cat has done little for the world. Old cat has been through the mill, peered at respectability and found that respectability has drawbacks.

So he has an appeal to me and to Wilmer and to Uncle Jake that a fluffy kitten or even an aristocratic Persian would never have. He has been there. Wherever "there" is, there he has been.

I suppose that is why Uncle Jake, who feels that everything inedible is a burden on the world, stands shivering in the doorway, calling, "Nice kitty, go out now, nice kitty . . . nice outside . . . beautiful outside . . . come on, kitty . . . nice kitty. . . . "

The addressed animal, meanwhile, takes two steps and sits down. He yawns and looks up. In his eyes can be seen his reaction. The reaction is, "Go chase yourself, you old goat. I'll go out when I get ready, but don't feed me any of this stupid slosh about the weather. It's a lousy night and you know it."

Wilmer has a more original but just as futile approach. Wilmer goes outside and kneels down in the snow on the porch and jangles his car keys. He says, "Come kitty, come kitty . . . see . . . fun out here . . . fun . . . come kitty."

The cat sits in the doorway with the heat at his back and leers at wet-kneed Wilmer.

"Roll over," I say. "Wilmer, roll over and maybe he'll come out to see if you're dead."

Sometimes I try to coax old cat outside with a bit of fish or a piece of ground beef. The only trouble with that method is that when I get him out and drop the stuff he grabs it and beats me to the hall again, where he sits eating what he wants and rubbing the rest into the floor.

Some day I am going to open the door and the cat will rush right out. That will be about Memorial Day, I think, unless Memorial Day is coolish or rainish.

But until he decides that he approves of the weather, we are going to have to fight the battle of the doorway every night. I guess we don't really mind. It's more educational than watching TV.

Of course, almost anything is.   ■

Thankful to Have Lived

There will be lists prepared and read to crowds and to congregations. There will be thanks for many things; for the freedoms sought for centuries and now attained in part; for the comforts that ease the harsher pains; for the progress toward all the goals that seemed for so long to be impractical dreams.

The lists will be long.

My thanks start with a simpler thing and yet a thing of wonder. I am thankful to have lived. When I was younger, I could be more specific. Now I see no need. The gift of life is so great that a person who gives proper thanks for it has no time to give thanks for anything else, anything else at all.

I am thankful to have lived and to be still living. I am thankful to be able to feel that I may live awhile longer. There are many things worth dying for and there have been things in the past for which I would have been willing to die. But I am glad that I did not die.

If the defense of personal and national freedom demands death in the future, then that will be the way it will be. One reason for being thankful for life is that life is thereby available to be given for a considered cause.

But even then, I will have lived, and for that living I am thankful. I have enjoyed living. There are people who say, "If we could see at birth what we have to go through in life, we would never dare to face it."

That is so wrong. That is so very wrong.

The frustrations and the pains, the losses and the miseries, the labor and the bitterness and the failures and the follies and

121

the shames. . . . all these were covered by the blanket of anticipation that eventually became reality. It has been so and it will
be so. A love that is mourned in its loss is a love that was once
glorious. It might have been more glorious, but it was glorious
enough. A friend who is gone is a friend who was once present.
It is only because he once meant so much that his absence is so
severely felt.

There is a classic cry of the thwarted young, of the "lost" generation, of the "beat" generation, of deprived boys and girls. It
is too often heeded by indulgent parents. It is a truth only because there was no alternative. There will never be an alternative.

But when they say, "I didn't ask to be born . . . " there is only
one real answer. That answer is, "You would have, had you been
able to."

When a man with a clear conscience says, "I'm not afraid to
die," he is telling the truth. He is not afraid. But he does regret
the need. He knows that intelligence fights always against igno-
rance and evil and that some men must die if the fight is to go on,
but he wishes it were otherwise. Fear is not the same as regret.

I am thankful to have lived. I am glad to have been here. That
is the basic. That is the foundation of thanks. Everything else is
embroidery. Thanks are due for food and shelter, for freedom
and for opportunity. Thanks are due for education and for
health and for friends and for family. But the greatest thanks are
for having been present to recognize their value.

So I am thankful for the gift of life. I have enjoyed every single
moment of it, even the moments of the completest misery, even
the agonies of the fiercest pains, even the black moods of
bitterness. I have always known that I preferred the light of an
anxious dawn to the continued blackness which postponed the
moment of truth. I don't mean that literally. I like the night. I like
the day. I like being a part of them both. For being that part, I am
thankful.

So that is that, on Thanksgiving Day, on any day, on every
day. I am thankful for having been. I am thankful to be. Simply
having been is complete compensation for the moments of
being which left the scars.   ■